Rock Bottom

(The Time Bubble Book 8)

By Jason Ayres

Cover art by:

Daniela Owergoor

http://dani-owergoor.deviantart.com/

For Natalie

Contents

Chapter One
December 2018

Kay was so drunk that she practically fell out of the front door of the pub. Just about managing to stay upright, she instinctively clutched at the clasp of her small, black, leather bag, desperate for a smoke.

It was chucking-out time at The Red Lion on a bitterly cold December night. The wind was howling all around her as she tottered around on her cheap high heels in a forlorn attempt to light her cigarette.

Cursing as the wind extinguished each attempt in a fraction of a second, she made for the doorway of the shop next door to seek some shelter. Cupping her hands around her mouth as she leant into the doorway, she finally managed to get the damned thing lit at the ninth time of asking.

Turning, she began to make her way along the town's main street, brightly lit by the same gaudy old Christmas lights that the council put up every year. There were drunken revellers everywhere, celebrating finishing work for the holidays. It was the last Friday night before Christmas, a night that she had heard the landlord of the pub refer to earlier in the evening as "Mad Friday".

A group of sexy young women dressed up in Santa outfits passed her by, laughing, followed by a group of young men, clearly hopeful of some action. They would all doubtless be heading for the town's only nightclub, keen to continue the festivities, but Kay had had enough. She had suffered enough humiliation for one night already.

Things had not gone well in her attempts to chat up various men in the pub and she couldn't face the likelihood of more rejection in the club commonly referred to by the locals as the "last chance saloon". It was said that if you couldn't pull in there, you couldn't pull anywhere and failure would be the final nail in the coffin of her already fragile confidence. Besides, she had work in the morning. Whatever else had gone wrong in her life lately, at least she still had a job.

Kay was so lonely that she had sunk to the stage where she would give herself to anyone who wanted to take her home. She did it in the hope that they would make her feel wanted for a few hours and with a vague hope that it might lead on to something more.

In reality, these liaisons rarely extended to even a few hours. Most of the men she managed to entice back to her flat were in and out in a matter of minutes. As soon as the deed was done, they were off back to their wives and girlfriends, satisfied now they had enjoyed their little bit of extra-curricular fun.

Her conquests, if she could call them that, were hardly trophies she could proudly display on the mantelpiece. They were pretty sad characters for the most part, fat and ugly middle-aged men who were only interested in her because they couldn't pull anyone else. Aware of her rapidly growing reputation as the "pub bike", they were drawn to her not for her fading looks but because they knew she was an easy lay.

She was just as aware of this as they were, but her self-esteem was so low she still allowed it to happen. The whole sorry situation had been going on for months.

But now, the offers were drying up. Kay knew she had let herself go to the point where even the desperadoes were looking elsewhere. She was forty-three years old but looked at least fifty. Years of excessive alcohol consumption to help her get through her miserable marriage had taken their toll. She had also taken up chain-smoking again since her husband had kicked her out, after nearly two decades of being smoke-free.

Living alone, she had seen her diet go rapidly downhill. With no motivation to cook any longer, most of her meals were takeaways, and she couldn't remember the last time she had eaten any fresh fruit or vegetables. All of these things had contributed to a rapid and premature ageing process. Her skin was blotchy and looked unhealthy, while her body was overweight and sagging in all the wrong places.

These were just the physical signs, but a lack of grooming and personal care had also contributed to the downward slide in her appearance. Things she had once taken for granted, like having her nails done or a trip to the hairdresser's, were now things of the past. She couldn't even afford to dye her hair anymore to keep the ravages of time at bay. Consequently, in a very short time her once beautiful blonde locks had become unkempt and greying.

3

She could see all this every time she looked in the mirror but tried to justify it to herself as being down to the inevitability of ageing. She couldn't say the same for the state of her teeth, however. She had been meticulous in looking after them throughout her life, with electric toothbrushes, regular dentist visits and lots of flossing. She had prided herself on reaching her forties without ever having to have as much as a filling.

Sadly, no amount of care could have prepared them for an extremely unpleasant incident that had taken place a couple of months ago. The wife of a man she'd taken home for a one-night stand had turned up the following day, hammering on the door of her flat.

When Kay hadn't answered, the woman kicked the front door in, easily shattering the flimsy lock, and then proceeded to beat the crap out of her, screaming obscenities as she went. Kay had no chance to explain that she hadn't known the man was married before the woman attacked her.

The man had conveniently forgotten to mention that he had a wife, but then they rarely did. Kay doubted that even if she had been given time to protest her innocence the woman would have taken any notice. Saying she didn't know was a pretty flimsy excuse after all.

By the time her assailant had mercifully departed, she had left Kay minus most of her front teeth. With no money for dental treatment in her impoverished state, she now had no choice but to go around looking like some horrible, toothless old crone. To top it all, her landlord, despite witnessing the

4

woman smashing in the door downstairs, still made Kay pay for a new lock.

Since she had lost the teeth, she had found men very hard to come by. Perhaps that in itself wasn't such a bad thing. Deep down, she felt quite disgusted with herself for taking men home with her to the extent that she had. There had been at least a dozen in the past eight months and none of them had satisfied her need to feel wanted in any way. All they had done was selfishly and emotionlessly thrust away inside her with not the slightest consideration of her needs.

They had been using her and she had been letting them do it. Kay knew things had to change, but she didn't know how. She was stuck in a rut and seemed incapable of breaking out of it. Most days she started with good intentions but nothing ever seemed to go her way. When every night was spent in the pub with the same old people, one day just merged into the next in one long cycle going round and round again. After a few drinks, any good intentions soon went out of the window.

For the past six months, she had been working in the town centre for a branch of a High Street chain of stores. She had started out on the tills, but she had been moved into the stockroom not long after she had lost her teeth. Her job now consisted primarily of locating and bringing out items that customers had ordered. Her manager had said she had been reassigned due to a reorganisation, but nobody else had been moved.

One day she was out of sight behind the back door on a cigarette break when she heard a couple of the other girls gossiping about her. They were joking that she wasn't allowed on the tills anymore because she was frightening the children. This had been incredibly hurtful but she didn't let on that she had heard them. She just wept quietly on the inside and got on with her work. She had thought the two girls were her friends, as they were always as nice as pie to her face, but it just went to show that she couldn't trust anyone.

Ever since then, she had felt paranoid about what people might be saying about her, leading her to live an increasingly reclusive lifestyle. She went to work and she went to the pub and that was the sum of her life. The first she had to go to or she would starve, the second was the only public place she felt comfortable in, and even then it took several vodkas before she could truly relax. At least in the pub, she was among those of a similar ilk, other losers and alcoholics, all drowning their souls together. If not exactly friends, at least she knew where she was with them.

Her job was minimum wage, soulless work which barely paid her rent, let alone anything else. Unable to face the world, on her days off she spent most of the day holed up in her flat until it was time to go to the pub. Recently, most nights had ended alone with her crying herself to sleep trying to figure out how and why her life had gone so wrong.

When she was eighteen, she had seemingly had it all. She was one of the brightest girls in her class and put it to good use in her exams, achieving three straight A's in her A levels.

She had stunning looks, too, having been blessed with a natural beauty and a lovely hourglass figure.

Not only did she have brains and looks, but she also had an easygoing, bubbly personality, too. It was rare for people to have all three of these things in abundance and it didn't go unnoticed. She was popular among the girls at school, all of whom wanted to hang out with her, but never abused that popularity by acting like some sort of queen bee.

As for the boys, they were swarming all over her in her later years of school. Most would have walked over hot coals if it had given them a chance to be her boyfriend. She resisted all offers, though, wanting to wait for the right one.

With offers from both Oxford and Cambridge, she seemingly had a glittering future ahead of her, but she wasn't in any hurry. Before leaving school she had already decided to put off going to university for a year to fulfil a desire to go travelling. Not only was this going to be an amazing adventure that would broaden her horizons, it also fitted in nicely with her long-term plans. Unlike many her age, she had very clear ideas about what she wanted to do with her life and how she was going to make it happen.

She was going to travel the world, and then return to do a degree in media studies. That wasn't something Oxford or Cambridge specialised in, but she had no qualms about going elsewhere to get the degree she wanted, even if those other universities didn't quite have the same prestige. She wasn't one for standing on ceremony.

7

She planned to work hard and make sure she graduated with top honours. Afterwards, she would forge a career in television, making and presenting travel documentaries around the world.

She could have undoubtedly achieved all of this had it not been for one fatal flaw in her character. Despite her high intellect, common sense and clear ambitions, she had a blind spot when it came to men. Waiting for the right one to come along had not worked out for her, and eventually, her hormones overcame those good intentions. From that point onwards her judgement in that area had been terrible, and she knew it.

Looking back, she could pinpoint the precise moment it had all started to go wrong. A bad choice of date for her end-of-term school ball had set in place a chain of events that had led to her being married with a baby by the time she was twenty-three.

Even that, she could have overcome and still forged that career later if she had married the right man, but she hadn't. Her choice of ball date had been unwise, but she didn't learn from that mistake. Her subsequent choice of husband had been nothing short of disastrous.

Dark, despairing thoughts swirled around in her mind as she struggled up the street, just like the few final, stray autumn leaves blowing around her ankles. The wind was from the east and directly in her face as she battled on through the bitter cold. Her attire of short, red skirt and skimpy leopard skin top provided scant protection against the elements. She had bought both cheaply in a charity shop, items that less than a year ago she would never have dreamt of wearing. They made her look like a slag and she knew it, but then everyone thought she was one anyway, so why bother to hide it?

The plastic advertising board for the local paper outside the newsagent was being severely buffeted in the wind and looked like it might blow over at any moment. "CHRISTMAS KILLER STRIKES AGAIN" screamed out at her from the board.

She passed a police van, the occupants uneasily keeping an eye on the noisy crowds emerging from Ye Olde Chapel, a chain pub at the other end of the town. From there it was only another couple of hundred yards, past a rockers' pub and an old men's pub, to the chip shop, above which lay her home of the past nine months.

The thought of yet another night ahead in the grubby little flat with its yellow-stained walls and the constant stench of fish filled her with gloom. The flat had been intended as a temporary stopgap. but there didn't seem to be any hope of her finding anywhere better anytime soon. Not with the way her estranged husband was deliberately dragging his heels over the divorce.

Although she had long reverted to her maiden name and referred to herself as a divorcee to anyone who might ask, she was technically still married. Her ex was making things as difficult for her as he possibly could, even by his standards.

The divorce proceedings which she had instigated several months before were dragging on and on. He had

9

painted a very convincing picture of her being an unfit mother during the negotiations, not only to his brief but also to their daughter. He had even gone to the extent of having a private detective follow her to rake up mud. Despite their separation, he was still making her life just as much a misery as he had when they had lived together.

Her heart sank when she saw how busy the chip shop was. There must have been at least twenty people packed into the relatively narrow customer area. There was no external entry to her flat – she had to go through to the back of the shop to a door marked "Private", the very door that her enraged assailant had kicked in before removing Kay's teeth.

Thankfully there was no sign of the owner, her hideous, obese and sluglike landlord, Mr McVie. His fish and chip empire stretched to two shops in the town and three others between here and Oxford. Mercifully he must be at one of the others tonight.

She had no desire to run into him. On top of her other woes, she was suffering serious financial problems, made worse by the extortionate amount of rent he charged her. She knew for a fact that there hadn't been enough money in her account this month to pay it and it had been due three days ago.

She entered the brightly lit shop, relieved to be out of the cold, and started to make her way through the groups of revellers who were eagerly clamouring for fat-laden protein and carbohydrates to soak up the alcohol they had drunk.

From the front door, she had to go all the way to the far end of the customer area, which took up the whole right-hand side of the shop. There were two doors at the end – the right-hand one of which led up to her flat.

The counter ran the whole length of the left-hand side of the shop. Kay herself felt hungry after her nightly skinful of booze, but the food in the glass displays didn't look particularly appetising. There were a couple of dried-up fish cakes that had probably been there for hours, a couple of battered sausages, and a single crusty, old pie.

Behind the counter, two or three young men busied themselves serving the drunken customers with their orders. Most were ordering kebabs which were always popular at this time of night. One of the men was busy slicing meat off what Kay always thought looked like a slowly rotating giraffe's neck. Another was taking a Hawaiian out of the pizza oven. It wasn't just a fish and chips shop. You could get almost every sort of fast food you could ever want at McVie's.

She had almost made it across to the back of the shop when she stumbled slightly, right in front of a group of rough-looking lads. Fearful of falling, she grabbed one of them for support but, far from being helpful, the lads cheered at her clumsiness. There were five or six of them, all in their mid-twenties. As she looked up at the face of the one she had grabbed hold of, she recognised the face. She had spoken to him earlier at the bar in The Red Lion.

One of his mates, a tall lad with spiky, blond hair and an earring, laughed and said, "Hey, Dave, isn't this that old slapper you were trying to chat up in the pub earlier?"

Dave, a fit, muscular guy who looked as if he seriously worked out, looked embarrassed. "Er, no, I don't think so..." he said.

His denial didn't do a lot for Kay's self-esteem.

"Don't fancy yours much, Dave!" shouted another one of the group.

The others all chortled, as Kay fumbled in her bag for the key to the newly installed Yale lock on the door. There was no way she wanted to get any food now; she just needed to get out of here. But the lads were blocking her way.

"Do you mind?" protested Kay. "I'm trying to get to my flat."

"So that's what the fishy smell was in the pub earlier," said the blond man. "Dave here said he thought it was your fanny."

"Go on, Dave, give her one," shouted another of the horrible men. "Maybe you'll get crabs – this is a fish and chips shop after all."

"Why don't you get her to give you a blowie, Dave?" shouted out yet another. "She'll probably be really good at it with no teeth to get in the way. I can't stand a woman that bites, can you?"

12

Laughter rang out all around, and not just from the men. The other customers were joining in, too. Her humiliation was well and truly complete. Finally locating her key, she forced her way through them and with relief managed to get the key to turn in the lock.

"The dentist isn't that way, love," said the blond man. "They're two doors down."

Everyone was laughing now, even the workers behind the counter. Not a single person in the shop had stood up for her. They had been like a baying pack of wolves, picking on the weakest.

She opened the door and rapidly closed it behind her. Then she staggered up the stairs, desperate to put distance between her and the sound of the men's laughter, still ringing in her ears. Entering the one-room bedsit, Kay sank down on her bed and wept. How could the men have been so cruel? How could her life have gone so wrong? She had never felt so alone.

She reached for the half-empty vodka bottle by her bed and took a swig. It was the only way she knew to blot out the misery.

Later, drugged by the massive amount of alcohol she had consumed, she slept. It was poor-quality sleep that would only leave her feeling worse in the morning.

She may have felt alone, but she was not unobserved. As she slept, there was a presence in the room, unseen and undetected by her. A spirit, one that another of the town's residents had once called an angel, had been watching over her.

Kay needed help, and the following day her angel would be waiting to start her on the road to recovery.

Chapter Two
December 2018

When she awoke she was cold from having kicked off the quilt. Her dreams had been vivid, haunted by the injustices of her past life. The last moments before she had woken up remained briefly imprinted on her mind. Her ex-husband and his dizzy, raven-headed girlfriend were laughing at her, just as the horrible men had done in the shop the previous evening.

"What did you ever see in her?" said Lucy, her hated ginger curls, which framed a pale, youthful complexion, cascading down around her shoulders.

"Stupid cow," said Alan, putting his arm around the girl who had replaced Kay, laughing as he did so.

It took a couple of seconds of consciousness for Kay to realise it was only a dream as her mind clicked back into the real world. A dream it may have been, but its origins were very much grounded in reality.

The last time she had seen Alan with Lucy had been in the street some weeks before. As soon as they had clocked her they had crossed the road, pretending they hadn't seen her. It was obvious that they had, as they made a big show of the fact they were holding hands, also turning to give each other an affectionate peck on the lips which they knew Kay couldn't fail to spot. Once they were past her, they burst into giggles, no doubt sharing some cruel joke at her expense.

The hurt Kay felt from her dream merely compounded the misery of the events of the previous evening. Thankfully, as her eyes adjusted to the dim light of the room and her hangover began to kick in, the memories, so vivid just a few moments before, swiftly burnt themselves out.

A grey light filtered through the partially closed curtains, illuminating her sad and dismal little room. She pulled the dirty and stained quilt back over herself in a forlorn attempt to get warm, but it was to no avail. She was still wearing the leopard skin top and knickers she had been dressed in the previous night, but even with them and the quilt, she felt much colder than usual. She looked across at her cheap digital clock radio, recently bought off the market. It was nearly half past eight and she was due in work at nine.

The flat she lived in consisted of one average-sized room and not a lot more. Her bed doubled as her sofa, and the remainder of her small living space was taken up by the kitchen if it could be called that. The cooking facilities amounted to two single electric rings with about a square metre of surface space on either side. There were two small cupboards above these two spaces, one of which was missing its door.

There was also a small sink taking up the space below the filthy window. It was so tiny, she couldn't even fit a washing-up bowl into it. When she had complained to Mr McVie about it, he had just laughed.

"What do you need to cook for when you've got a perfectly good chip shop downstairs?" he had said in his broad Glaswegian accent.

That was pretty much par for the course where McVie was concerned. She had quickly learnt that it was pointless complaining to him about anything. He never fixed anything.

The only other notable piece of furniture was an ageing MFI chest of drawers that she had bought second-hand from a charity shop. All of her clothes were stuffed into the three small drawers, two of which were sagging as the wafer-thin pieces of baseboard collapsed under the weight. She had tried supergluing the boards back in place, but they soon came unstuck again. Most of the fake wood veneer had peeled off the top. It was amazing it had lasted as long as it had, which was more than could be said for the company that had made it.

As for washing her clothes, that was out of the question. Her flat hadn't come equipped with a washing machine, and even if she had been able to afford one, there was nowhere to fit it. So she had to go to the launderette, up on one of the rough estates in the older part of town.

She was forever running out of clean clothes and had lowered her standards considerably. Now she wore underwear two days in a row, tops for three or four, and jeans for up to two weeks at a time. She figured the longer she could eke her clothes out, the less money and time she would have to spend in the launderette which doubled as the town's main drug-dealing hub. She hated going there.

For someone who had once taken such pride in her appearance, it was a shocking state of affairs. It was all down to one simple problem: lack of money.

She knew she was in a mess but with the current financial situation, she just didn't know how she was going to drag herself out of it. If she could have weaned herself off the fags and booze it would have made a significant difference to her finances, but she just didn't have the willpower or the inclination to break those habits at present. Life had become so intolerable she needed to drown her sorrows in the pub every night just to keep going.

As she lay in bed this Saturday morning, wrapping the quilt around her in a tight cocoon, she thought about the situation she was in and what had led her there. Should she be trying to work out where she had gone wrong and what she could do to change things, or was she being harsh blaming it all on herself? Should she instead be focusing her thoughts on who else had played a part?

She didn't think of herself as a bitter and twisted woman, blaming everyone else for her own shortcomings, but it was hard not to point the finger when she thought about her ex-husband, Alan Phipps. How she wished she had never met him. How much different would her life have been without him? Much better, undoubtedly.

But wishing she had never met him was a double-edged sword. If she hadn't, then she wouldn't have her daughter. She may have married someone else and had other children, but they wouldn't be Maddie. Other children were an abstract concept: doubtless, she would have loved them, but they weren't real. Maddie was: she was flesh and blood, made uniquely out of bits of her, and Alan and she couldn't bear the thought of being without her.

But the sad reality of the current situation was that she was without her. It was less than a week until Christmas and Kay hadn't heard from Maddie since late September when term had started at Durham University.

Durham: one of the places where I could have gone, thought Kay. It was an opportunity long gone, a ship that had sailed without her in the long-lost world that was her past.

Why hadn't she heard from Maddie? For the same reason she hadn't heard from many other people in the family. Alan had poisoned her mind against her. He was very good at doing that.

Kay had seen domestic violence portrayed on television, but Alan was far more subtle than that. He had never laid a finger on her, but bit by bit over time he had ground her down into submission. A little put-down there, a little bit of freedom taken away there: gradually and almost imperceptibly, he had whittled away her personality and her strength.

Eventually, when he had no more use for her, he had tossed her aside like half an orange, every last drop of juice sucked out of her. She hadn't even realised it was happening until it was too late. It was only now, in hindsight, that she could see exactly what he had done to her.

19

If she had been the victim of domestic violence, at least she could have done something about it. She could have gone to the police and got him locked up. But the types of wounds Alan inflicted left no scars – none that could be seen, anyway. Nobody else could see what he had done to her, which quickly became apparent during the breakup.

After he had kicked her out of the marital home, she had tried to confide in one of her friends, the wife of another couple that the two of them sometimes socialised with. It was quickly obvious that the woman was only paying lip service to her grievances. She didn't believe what Kay was saying, and why would she? Alan was always so charming and so reasonable with everyone he met. He dressed smartly and always said and did the right thing. It was an act he put on for the world and one he had long ago perfected. No one saw what really went on behind closed doors.

Kay was determined to try and make sense of it all in her mind. She was never going to sort herself out until she could come to terms with how she had ended up in this situation in the first place. She thought back, far back into the past, to the time just before she had met Alan. What had led her to be so easily taken in by him?

She had met him in the spring of 1995 when she was nineteen years old and on her gap year while she decided which university she was going to. She had several offers on the table. With her grades and sparkling recommendation from the school, they were all happy to defer her entry for a year.

She never made it. A chain of seemingly random events and decisions over the preceding months had led her to fall into a relationship with Alan. From then on he had ensured that the door leading to higher education was slowly and quietly closed.

Around the time she had left school the previous summer she had lost her virginity with a Jack the Lad character called Glen. He turned out to be her first, but certainly not the last, seriously bad choice of man.

She hadn't wanted to go out with him in the first place, much preferring his friend Richard, but Glen had told her that Richard was gay and muscled his way in instead. What he had said about Richard was eventually revealed to have been a lie, many years later.

Before long, she had good reason to seriously regret getting involved with Glen. Before Christmas of the same year, she had fallen pregnant. A few weeks after they had been going out, Glen refused to use condoms anymore, claiming that he was allergic to them. He insisted that she go on the Pill instead. Somehow during the crossover period she had conceived.

Far from being supportive, Glen had ordered her to "get rid of it", informing her that he had no intention of becoming a dad at his age. She was left in no doubt whatsoever as to the ultimatum she was facing – it was him or the kid.

He was no help to her whatsoever during the whole process. Then, once her baby was dead, he promptly turned around and dumped her anyway. Not long after that, she discovered he had been sleeping with at least two other girls behind her back for months. This included the very day when she was having the abortion when he claimed he couldn't get the day off work. She later found out that he had actually been busy in bed with a barmaid from Ye Olde Chapel, no doubt spinning the same bullshit about being allergic to latex.

Losing a baby and being let down at such a tender age hit Kay hard. The feeling of invincibility that her youth and early academic success had given her was stripped away by the whole sordid state of affairs. Real life had come right up in front of her and well and truly slapped her in the face.

In the dark winter months of early 1995, she sank into her first and only bout of teenage depression. She had been working flat out in the weeks leading up to Christmas in a temporary job at the local sorting office, but it was only seasonal work. Once all the Christmas post was sorted and sent she was no longer needed. Now she found herself lacking the desire to seek more work and barely left the house in January and February.

As the nights drew out and the weather got warmer, she picked herself up and dusted herself down. She was determined not to waste the rest of her year off. With Glen out of the way, she could at least now revisit her earlier plans to go travelling. But not earning any money for the first two months of the year had put a dent in her finances.

Needing to earn some decent money to finance her plans, she decided to sign up with a temp agency for a few months. If she got enough money together she could head off in June and still be away for over three months. That was not as long as she had originally planned, but even so, there was plenty she could do in three months.

There were many temp agencies for her to choose from, offering different types of work. She decided to go for one that specialised in office work. Working in an office was not something she aspired to, but she didn't think it would do any harm to get a couple of months' experience in that sphere. It would be something she could stick onto her CV after university. Competition for jobs at the BBC and Channel 4 would be fierce. She needed to give herself the best possible chance if she was to get to where she wanted to be.

This seemingly unimportant choice of agency at the time was one of many minor decisions that had led her to where she was today. Kay reflected that life was probably like that for most people, their whole lives mapped out via a series of random events and choices.

The first, and as it turned out the only, place the agency sent her was a large, grey building on the outskirts of Oxford. It was the head office of one of Britain's largest supermarket chains, and she was to provide maternity cover for a clerk in the accounts department.

It was a dull, repetitive job which reaffirmed her desire to make something of herself. She could face a few weeks of doing this sort of work, but to do it for a whole lifetime would have been soul-destroying.

Part of her job involved cashing cheques for staff. This was still a popular way of paying for things, as well as acquiring currency back in those days. This meant she came into contact with a lot of people in the business, especially toward the end of the month. Then everyone started cashing cheques a couple of days before payday, knowing they wouldn't reach their accounts before their wages went in.

Her pretty looks didn't go unnoticed and she frequently found herself being chatted up by the male employees. They were delighted to find an attractive nineteen-year-old girl manning the desk. Kay didn't know it, but she was a popular topic of conversation among the men in the office who referred to her as "fresh meat", some even placing bets on who could bed her first.

One man, in particular, seemed smitten by her, which was pretty obvious from the number of visits he made to the accounts department. By the end of her second week, he was visiting the desk to cash small cheques on a daily basis.

She didn't know it then, but this man was to become her future husband. Alan was much older than her, just turned thirty and a rising star within the organisation. He had just been part of the marketing team that had successfully launched the chain's first loyalty card scheme, giving points to shoppers for their food purchases. As a result, he had been rewarded with a new role as a buyer in the wine department.

He was smart, attractive and confident. He was also a great deal more mature than some of the younger lads in the office who had made clumsy attempts to ask her out. When he asked her if she would like to come out for lunch with him, it seemed almost rude to say no. She also couldn't deny that she was flattered by his charm and interest in her.

Lunch led on to dinner dates, and a host of other romantic gestures. When he told her he was going to France for a few days on a wine buying trip and asked if she would like to accompany him as his assistant, she leapt at the chance.

They spent three wonderful days in the Champagne region in the spring sunshine, all expenses paid, during which they inevitably became lovers. And what a lover he turned out to be – accomplished, confident and generous in bed, a million miles away from Glen's clumsy and selfish fumbling. She was well and truly smitten.

When they returned to the UK he asked her to move in with him. Her parents were opposed to the idea, but she was lovestruck and ignored them. What did they know? Just six weeks after meeting Alan, she packed a suitcase full of clothes and moved in with him.

Nearly a quarter of a century later she would find herself packing a suitcase again, but this time it was when he was showing her the door. There were no parents to run back to by then: they were both dead. Meanwhile, he was moving Lucy in – another young employee. The wheel had turned full circle.

Those first few months living with Alan were blissful. He was doing very well for himself, living already in a spacious semi-detached house. In those early days, they spent every waking hour together. He drove her into work every day in his company Volvo, and then they met for lunch, sometimes sneaking off to Shotover, a local beauty spot, for a bit of naughty fun in the car.

In the evening he would drive her home again. They would prepare gourmet meals together in the kitchen, washing them down with the fine wines that he acquired as a perk of his job. Later they would watch movies and make love on the sofa. He had all the satellite channels, something she had never had at home. Her parents were of a generation who considered that four TV channels were quite sufficient.

Alan was generous to a T back then, never asking her to contribute a penny towards the food or bills. He made life as easy as he possibly could for her, which made it all the more difficult to face the decision that was looming on the horizon.

Living scot-free had enabled her to save money rapidly for the travelling she hoped to do in the summer, but she was now facing a dilemma about whether or not she should go. She had told Alan of her plans to go travelling when they had been away in France but had avoided discussing it since she had moved in with him. He had not mentioned it again either, which didn't help. Perhaps he had just assumed that now she was living with him, she had dropped her plans. The trouble was, the longer she left it, the harder she was finding it to bring the subject up.

Further ahead, there was also the issue of university that would have to be tackled at some point. She had told him all about her career plans on one of their first meals out. He had seemed enthusiastic and encouraging, but again it had not been mentioned since. Now she was at the point where she needed to

26

accept a place if she was going that September. She knew she couldn't stay in Oxford with him unless she changed her course to something they offered, which she was not willing to do. She still had her heart set on media studies and was strongly considering Leeds or Durham as her best options.

Alan had made her feel so wanted and happy that she was getting strong feelings of guilt over her plans. Would leaving him to travel or study be an act of betrayal after all he had done for her? If there had been any cracks in their relationship at that time then she would at least have had some reason to justify leaving, but he was just so damned perfect. That was going to make it all the harder to leave.

With the benefit of decades of hindsight, Kay now wondered if he had been manipulating her even back then. She had assumed then that he hadn't asked about her plans because he had forgotten about them, but was he just playing a clever game with her? Had he been so nice to her purely so that she would feel unable to leave?

His impeccable conduct back then was a far cry from what she was to experience in later years, once he had got her where he wanted her. But she was only nineteen then. She simply didn't have the life experience to see what he was doing. Maybe there had been warning signs that her forty-three-year-old self would have spotted a mile off, but she was young and in love, and as she had heard people say many times, love is blind.

Spring gave way to summer, and as June dawned she knew she could not put off her decisions any longer. Breaking away from Alan would be very hard but she had saved for and planned her trip around Europe for so long that she couldn't turn her back on it now. It didn't have to spell the end of the relationship – if he loved her, he would wait for her to come back – wouldn't he?

She had over £3,000 in the bank and a clear plan in her mind as to what she wanted to do. She planned to start at the top of Europe and work her way downwards.

She had decided that one of the Scandinavian countries would be her first destination, with mid-June as her planned departure date. This wasn't a date she had chosen at random. A year or two before, she had watched the latest David Attenborough series, *Life in the Freezer*, on BBC1. She found it fascinating to learn how the sun never set in the summer in the Arctic regions.

She had vowed there and then that she would one day go and see the midnight sun. Hence her rather unusual choice of country to begin her travels through Europe. By choosing a date as close as possible to the summer solstice, she wouldn't have to travel all the way to the North Pole. All she had to do was get inside the Arctic Circle. Her best options for this seemed to be Norway or Finland.

She had opted for Finland. This gave her the option to visit Lapland, somewhere she had seen depicted in many Christmas movies. She doubted it would seem very Christmassy in June, but no matter. She would get a budget flight to Helsinki, and from there travel north to the city of Rovaniemi. She would give herself the best possible chance of seeing the midnight sun by ensuring she was there on the date of the summer solstice. Then she just had to keep her fingers crossed for a sunny day.

From there she would travel south by train using a student railcard. She would visit as many countries as she could, finishing with a tour of the Greek islands in September. She had built up a good selection of guidebooks to help her find the youth hostels where she would stay and the places of interest she could visit.

It would mean lugging a lot of books around with her, but that was how people did things in those days. It was 1995 and the internet revolution was only just beginning. Online guides, the few that existed, were in their infancy and the only way to access them would be in one of the internet cafés which were springing up all over the place at that time.

It would be an exciting time to be travelling in Europe. The Iron Curtain had recently come down and there were a host of newly independent states springing up, formerly part of the Soviet Union. These had once been very difficult to visit but were now throwing open their borders, keenly embracing and welcoming visitors from the Western world.

Kay hoped to include some of these on her journey. Everyone else went to France, Spain and Italy, but she wanted to do something different, something unusual. It was going to be the adventure of a lifetime.

The thought that she was just nineteen, inexperienced and potentially vulnerable, didn't dissuade her. She was young and fearless, her heart and mind full of adventure. To her, this would only be the start – one day she planned to be the one writing the guidebooks rather than reading them.

But none of it ever happened.

She kept putting off telling Alan, even booking her flight before broaching the subject with him. On the same day she booked the flight she also accepted a place at Leeds University. She didn't tell him about that either.

It was just four days before she was due to fly from Heathrow to Helsinki on the third Saturday in June when she finally plucked up the courage to tell him. She hadn't expected him to take it well, but he was surprisingly supportive. He even offered to drive her to the airport the night before and pay for them to spend a last night together in a hotel, before seeing her off in the morning. He was so nice and reasonable about everything, she hadn't for a moment thought of turning his offer down.

That was her first mistake. Had he got angry or upset at that point, it would have been easier to break away. Kay would still have had a few days to get her act together for her trip. But he had been one step ahead of her all the way. She was sure now that he had known exactly what he had been doing to turn the situation to his advantage. She had seen many similar examples of his cunning in the intervening years. Unfortunately, back then she had still been blissfully unaware of how he operated.

It was just one of so many "what if?" moments she had played over and over in her mind in the long, lonely hours she had spent in her flat lately. The morning she had been due to fly from the airport was one of the pivotal moments. That one wrong decision she had made that day had followed her down the years, like a lead weight dragging behind her.

She had let him talk her out of going at the eleventh hour and after that, the opportunity never arose again. He had got his own way and it would set a precedent for the rest of their relationship. Without realising it, she had already become subservient to him.

Twenty-five years on, she had still not seen the midnight sun. It seemed there was precious little chance now that she ever would.

Chapter Three
December 2018

Wearily Kay dragged herself out of bed, trying feebly to gather the strength to face another day.

It wasn't far to the bathroom if it could even be called that. It was a tiny room with a toilet in one corner and a shower cubicle she could barely squeeze into in another. There was also a sink, even smaller than the one in the kitchen. There was no towel rail – the only place she could hang a towel was over the back of the door.

That was her luxury en suite bathroom, as McVie had outrageously called it when he first showed her around. It wasn't even a proper room. The wall separating it from her bedroom was just a cheap partition, of the type used in offices to separate conference rooms, and it wobbled when she walked across the floor.

The faded yellow ceramic tiles, ingrained with decades of other people's dirt, were icy to the touch. The cold was a shock to her feet after the threadbare grey carpet of the bedroom which at least provided a smidgeon of warmth.

Avoiding the tile with the large crack running diagonally across it, she fumbled for the shower controls. As fast as she could she reached for the left-hand control, turning it clockwise and quickly pulling her hand back. She wasn't quick enough, and got a splash of cold water across her arm, just as she did every other day. The shower head was ancient and clogged up with black mould. Rather than one continuous flow, it sprayed what little water it gave out in all sorts of unpredictable directions.

While she was waiting for the hot water to come through, she kicked off her skanky T-shirt and knickers, eager to feel the relief of the hot shower as she shivered in the cold.

It was colder in the room than usual, even accounting for the freezing weather outside. She was soon to find out why. As she stepped into the shower she got a much bigger shock than the one the tiles had given to her feet. The water was icy cold. She gasped for breath and quickly stepped back, catching the big toe of her right foot in the cracked tile, giving it a nasty pinch.

"For fuck's sake!" she shouted out in frustration. It was just one thing after another. She had just about had enough of this miserable existence. As so often in recent days, dark thoughts filled her mind as her eyes welled up with tears once again.

And then she caught sight of herself in the mirror above the sink. The cold tiles and cold water may have given her body a shock, but that was nothing in comparison to the surprise that now greeted her eyes.

Looking back at her from the mirror was not the tired, tear-stained face of despair that she could barely bring herself to look at these days. Instead, she saw a vision of youth and beauty that she instantly recognised as her own. Only a few moments ago she had been lying in bed thinking all about that pretty girl she used to be, and now here she was, looking right back at her.

Before she had a chance to ponder why she might be seeing the image of her younger self in the mirror, she had something else to think about. A split second after she had first set eyes on the reflection, it spoke.

"So you recognise me, then?" said her younger self in clear, unbroken tones.

"What? How?" croaked Kay, incredulously, her voice dry and rough from last night's smoking and drinking. She couldn't even begin to contemplate how this could be happening or why. Before she could even begin to try and make sense of the situation, the image from long ago spoke again.

"Let me put your mind at rest and save us the routine of going through the usual questions," replied her youthful reflection. "You're not dreaming, hallucinating or mad. I'm not your younger self, just a projection of her, to remind you who you used to be. There is nothing to be afraid of. I've come here to help you."

"How?" asked Kay again, so gobsmacked by this strange turn of events that she was unable to muster any more than this monosyllabic response.

"Well, I suggest you think of me as your guardian angel," replied her reflection. "That was the moniker another lost soul I helped recently gave me and I rather like it. I have been given a lot of different names in my time. Another I visited long ago dubbed me 'The Ghost of Christmas Past'. I think that's quite appropriate, given the time of year, don't you think?"

Kay couldn't even fashion a single-word response this time, as her hung-over mind wrestled with making sense of this bizarre situation.

"I can see you're confused," said the angel. "So let's make this easy. I've come to help you like I said before. I can see life's gone very wrong for you and I want to give you the chance to confront your inner demons. I know all about what happened in your past – about your failed marriage and how your life didn't turn out as you had hoped."

Finding her voice, Kay replied, "How do you know?"

"I can see inside your mind," replied the angel. "I was reading your thoughts as you lay in bed this morning. And I saw what happened downstairs last night. I can pretty much see everything. I have the ability to travel to any and every point in time and space simultaneously and see the potential result of every decision ever made. Though in practice, that gets a bit tiring even for me. It's a case of serious information overload if I try and do too much at once."

"How?" asked Kay once again.

"That seems to be your favourite word this morning," replied the angel. "Don't worry about the how because it's beyond your comprehension. Just accept what I'm telling you and then we can move on."

Kay quickly decided that she might as well accept it, even though the whole thing was preposterous. Maybe she was going crazy, but things could not get any worse than they already were, so why not go along with it?

Perhaps going crazy would be a relief. If she was so fucked up now that she was losing her grip on the car crash that was her life, perhaps it would be a blessed relief. At least if she got carted off by the men in white coats there would be someone to look after her then.

But in the seemingly unlikely event that this truly was some sort of miraculous visitation, she may as well grab firm hold of whatever it had to offer. This angel had said she had come to help her, after all, and what did she have to lose? There wasn't a lot left to lose in her life: she had lost it all already.

"OK, I accept it," she said. "So what happens next?"

"It's pretty simple. I'm going to let you live six days of your life over again. Any six days you like but I must clarify, they need to be in the past."

The angel specified that because another lost soul she had recently visited had unexpectedly asked to see his own future, which had annoyed her no end. Even despite her all-knowing, all-powerful presence, she took her eye off the ball occasionally and hadn't seen that one coming. Being caught out by a mere mortal was humiliating.

"That's it?" replied Kay, feeling somewhat underwhelmed. "How's that going to help me?"

"Think about it," replied the angel. "It will give you the chance to revisit some of those pivotal moments in your life and perhaps do them differently."

"OK, I get it," said Kay, her mind opening up to the possibilities. "So I could go back in time to the day my ex-husband first asked me out and tell him to get lost?"

"You could do that," replied the angel. "But it would be a bit of a waste of a day, wouldn't it?"

"No, I don't think so. Because then my whole life would change," said Kay excitedly. "Without that sod, I could live the life I always wanted to."

"Actually, no, you can't," replied the angel. "I'm glad you brought this up as it saves any misunderstandings later on. I'm afraid I can't allow you to change anything in the past. When you travel back to the past, the day you will visit will be a temporary copy, nothing more. When you return to the present, that copy will cease to exist."

"What's the bloody point of that?" protested Kay. "That's no use to me whatsoever. When I get back here, I'll just be back to square one."

"That's what most people think, to begin with," replied the angel. "But it's all in the application. You can do a lot in a day if you put your mind to it. There are all sorts of possibilities. Maybe you cannot change history but you can resolve some of the burning issues that have been eating away at your soul. Generally, people find when it's all over they are in a much better place to take their lives forward."

"Everyone?" asked Kay.

"Pretty much," said the angel. "Most are sceptical, to begin with, and unsure of what to do, but no one's ever turned down the offer. There are no strings attached, no consequences, just a once-in-a-million-lifetimes, six-day trip back through your past. It's an experience very few will ever have and something money can't buy. It's not something you can book down at Thomas Cook."

"Why six days?" asked Kay. "Why not five or seven?"

"I've found six to be the optimum number for people. It's enough for them to do the things they need to do, but not so many that they waste days. So six days it is – use them wisely."

"But where to begin?" asked Kay, beginning to warm to the idea. "The possibilities are endless."

"Most people struggle with their first choice so I normally give them a little helping hand to get started," replied the angel.

"I could certainly use one," replied Kay, feeling like a kid in a sweet shop not knowing where to start.

"How about this?" suggested the angel. "Do you remember what you were thinking about just before I arrived? Not the part about freezing your tits off in the shower and hurting your foot, but what you were thinking about before you got out of bed?"

"Yes," replied Kay. "I was thinking about the day Alan talked me out of flying to Finland."

"Well, there you go, then," said the angel. "That's your first port of call. Go and see the midnight sun. You've always regretted not going, so now's your chance."

"That's an awesome idea," replied Kay. "You're right: I always regretted not taking that trip. The only thing is, I can't remember the exact date. All I know is it was June 1995, just before the solstice."

"Don't worry about the details," said the angel. "You don't have to programme the date into a computer or anything. I already checked back to the date of your flight. It was Saturday 17th June 1995. I also took the liberty of checking the weather forecast and I'm pleased to report that it was clear and sunny that night in Rovaniemi. All you've got to do is make it there in one day. It's going to be quite a challenge but it's definitely achievable and will be all the more fun for it. As for your other five trips, well, you'll have plenty of time when you are travelling to think about what you want to do with them."

Kay was very excited at the prospect ahead. She could leave her current woes behind her, if only for a day, and contemplate the voyage of self-discovery that lay before her. She had better get herself ready.

"Shouldn't I put some clothes on first?" she asked, suddenly noticing that she was shivering. She had become oblivious to the cold, so distracted had she been by the bizarre conversation of the last few minutes.

"No need," replied the angel, "You're going back into your old body and your old clothes. You can't take anything from here back with you. So, are you ready?"

"No time like the present," said Kay, and then quipped, "Or do I mean the past?" It was the first time she had felt in good humour for weeks. If all this was for real, she was about to go on an unprecedented adventure and she couldn't wait to get started.

"How does it work?" she added.

"Like this," said the angel. She winked at Kay from the mirror and the room around her dissolved into nothingness.

Chapter Four
June 1995

The next thing Kay was aware of was that she was back in bed, waking sharply as if from a vivid dream, just as she had when waking in the flat an hour or so earlier.

For the first second or two, that was what she thought had happened. She had dreamt all this as well. She might have known it was too good to be true.

A second or two after that, as consciousness took proper hold, she realised that things were not as they should be. For a start, she was warm and the bed was incredibly comfortable, not at all like the horrible, stained and flea-bitten mattress she had to make do with in the flat. Not only that, someone was snoring beside her.

She had been drunk last night, just like every other night, but not so drunk that she wouldn't have remembered taking someone home with her. It was such a rare event of late that there was no way she would have forgotten it. But there was certainly somebody beside her. She couldn't see who, as it was extremely dark in the room.

But this wasn't the night after last night, she reminded herself. If the angel had come true with her promise, it was over twenty-three years ago. This wasn't her bedroom in the flat, of that she was certain. It was never this warm, even when the heating was working. If it really was Saturday 17th June

1995 then she was pretty sure she knew where she was, but it was too dark for her to confirm at the moment.

She got up out of bed and headed over towards a tiny glimmer of light, high up in the room where she could see the join of the curtains. As she made her way across the room she realised that not only did she not have a hangover, but she also felt extremely light on her feet.

She pulled the curtains apart and was greeted by glorious early morning sunshine, bathing the front of an airport terminal. There was no doubting where she was now – she was in the hotel at Heathrow where she had spent the night before she had been due to fly to Helsinki.

The shafts of sunlight penetrated across the room to the sleeping figure on the bed. She already knew who it would be before she even turned to make the confirmation. There he was, the man she loathed, back in the days when she thought the sun shone out of his arse.

Now it was shining on his arse which was sticking out of the side of the bed. She was pleased to see that opening the curtains hadn't woken him up. It gave her time to think about what she was going to do.

She caught a glimpse of herself in the full-length mirror on the front of the wardrobe. Again she saw the youthful image of herself that the angel had appeared as in her flat. But this time it was a true reflection of her as she was at this moment. She stood for a while and gazed upon her young, perfect body.

"What fantastic tits I used to have," she murmured out loud. She cupped them both in her hands, revelling in how full and firm they were. She felt herself starting to get horny and quickly let go, trying to suppress a succession of erotic thoughts that suddenly crept into her mind.

She had forgotten how high her libido had been when she had been young. She looked across at Alan, remembering how they hadn't been able to keep their hands off each other in those early days of their relationship.

Later, when she had grown to despise him, she couldn't bear to have him anywhere near her, not that it was ever a problem. He had long since embarked on a string of affairs by that time and no longer had any desire for her.

Looking at him now, her head was filled with conflicting emotions. This Alan in front of her wasn't the bastard she had grown to hate, he was the younger one she had adored and lusted after. With hormones surging through her youthful body, she felt long-forgotten desires resurfacing within her. Could she blame this younger Alan for his sins of later years?

"Get a grip," she said to her reflection, even though this version couldn't talk back. "Come on, Kay, think with the contents of your brains, not your knickers."

She swiftly reminded herself that Alan was a bastard and always had been. Any glorious honeymoon period she may have enjoyed with him had been based on his deception and lies. She had allowed her lust for him and her inexperience

43

with adult relationships to blind her to his true nature. If she touched him now, she would be betraying herself all over again.

He stirred, rolling over and opening his eyes.

"Morning, gorgeous," he said. "What time is it?"

She glanced at the clock on the bedside table. "Nearly twenty to six," she replied.

"Come back to bed," he said, pulling back the covers to leave her in no doubt as to his intentions. "There's plenty of time before you check in."

"I can't," she replied. "I've just come on." It was an easy lie and one she had used plenty of times before. He always accepted it.

"Can you sort me out, then?" he asked hopefully.

"I think you had more than enough last night," she replied, based on vague memories from nearly a quarter of a century ago. She tried to make it sound light-hearted. She didn't want him to have any reason to suspect she was not who she appeared to be. Later he was going to try and stop her from getting on the plane. She didn't want to say anything now that might make him want to bring those plans forward.

The memories of that morning were flooding back to her now. Quickly, she formed a rough plan of what she needed to do. All she had to do was act normally until she got inside the airport. Once they were surrounded by people, there was no way he would be able to stop her. Here, where they were in private, he could.

He looked disappointed at the lack of sex but didn't push the issue and went into the bathroom. It gave Kay time to familiarise herself with her surroundings, paying particular attention to her luggage.

There was a large, red rucksack in the room, stuffed full of everything she needed for the next three months. There was also a smaller, denim handbag, which she immediately went for.

It contained her purse, a notebook, a pen, and various make-up and sanitary items. Her flight tickets were also there, together with her passport, the old-fashioned, black, pre-EU edition. She quickly double-checked the flight and check-in times. She could check in from ten past six, so there wouldn't be long to wait. The sooner she was shot of Alan, the better.

She felt as if something was missing from the bag as she rummaged through, and then she realised what it was. There was no mobile phone. Of course, there wouldn't be. She didn't have one. Very few people in 1995 did. How strange it was going to seem, living in a world where there was no internet, no Facebook, and no way at all to quickly communicate with the wider world. How on earth had people managed to stay in touch with each other?

Then again, maybe it was a good thing. She liked the idea of nobody knowing where she was or being able to get hold of her. It seemed bold, even dangerous, by modern standards.

She knew she had a camera in her rucksack and lots of rolls of film, ready to photograph anything and everything on her trip. It would be odd not uploading them straight to Facebook. In this time period, it would be a case of keeping the films until she got back to the UK and then taking them down to Boots to be developed.

Ruefully she reflected that there would be no point taking any photos of the midnight sun, as she wouldn't get the chance to show them to anyone. If she had interpreted what the angel had told her correctly, by tomorrow she would be back in 2018 and it would be as if none of this had ever happened. She was pretty sure she wouldn't find a twenty-three-year-old Kodak film case in her pocket when she got home.

After Alan had finished in the bathroom she took a long, hot shower and luxuriated in the fast, powerful streams of water. It was way better than the pathetic excuse she had for a shower in the flat, which was more like a garden sprinkler than a power shower, which was what McVie had laughably called it. Even when she did have hot water, it was difficult to get enough of it onto her to keep warm.

She worried that Alan might try and come and molest her in the shower, but her fears were unfounded. He generally kept his distance from her when she was on her period. Thankfully she wasn't, but he wasn't to know that. She didn't want that inconvenience to deal with if she was going to be travelling all day.

When she was finished in the shower, she wrapped a towel around herself and made her way back to the bedroom. She tried not to make it too obvious that she felt uneasy at him looking at her naked body and made sure she dressed quickly. The sooner she got out of this hotel room and into the terminal building, the better.

She indulged in a little small talk as they crossed the road to the terminal, anxious to get this over with as quickly as possible. He was rambling on about some big golf tournament going on in America, something she had not the remotest interest in, but she feigned interest just to pass the time. She hadn't remembered him being this boring. Perhaps she had just been too busy enjoying all the sex at the time to notice. Well, she was certainly noticing now.

"Yeah, this new golfer, Tiger Woods, he's playing in his first US Open this weekend," he said. "They reckon he's going to be something special."

Although she hated golf, she had of course heard of Tiger Woods. She couldn't not have, as Alan had idolised him and gone on about him all the time.

Thankfully the check-in queue was not long at this early hour and she soon was free of her rucksack, watching it disappear on the conveyer. There was an hour and a half left until the flight.

"I really ought to be getting through to the other side," she said.

"Don't go just yet, darling," said Alan. "I don't want to be separated from you until I absolutely have to. Come on, let's go and grab a coffee."

This was word for word what he had said the first time she had been here. The word "darling" grated with her, but she had to smile and go along with it. She knew what was to come, and when it did, she'd be prepared, unlike last time.

Sure enough, as soon as they were seated, it started.

"I can't believe you're really going," he said. "I love you so much, I can't bear the thought of being parted from you for one day, let alone three months."

"I know," she replied. "But the time will fly by, you'll see. And when I come back, we can be together all the time."

In Kay's current mindset, that was a total lie, but she was sticking to the script for the moment. Although it would have been easier to just get up and walk off with the minimum of fuss, she wanted to see him beg pathetically, just like he had before. But this time she would not cave in.

Suddenly he began blubbing uncontrollably, like a baby.

"Please don't go, Kay," he pleaded. "I love you. I can't live without you."

This was so typical, she thought. It was all about him and his feelings. It was alright for him, he had his career and his fancy job travelling around vineyards, but what about her plans and her dreams? He had never cared about any of that. All he cared about was how it would affect him.

"You know I've got my heart set on this trip, Alan. I've dreamt of doing it since I was fifteen."

"Please, Kay, I'll do anything. You can still travel. Look, I went down to the travel agents earlier in the week and booked us this."

He pulled some tickets out of his bag and showed them to her. She didn't even need to look at them to know what they were. She had been through all of this before. It was a package holiday for two to the Algarve.

"Two weeks in the sun, just me and you together. I'll pay for everything, don't worry, and you can go travelling later. Or better still, I'll get a sabbatical from work and we'll go travelling together."

This was the point at which she had capitulated before but she wasn't going to be fooled a second time. He never did let her go travelling, despite several attempts on her part to rearrange it. The sabbatical of course never happened – apparently, he was too indispensable at work to be spared. Not long after that, he had talked her out of going to university as well by fixing her up with a full-time job in his department.

As for the holiday in the Algarve, on the first day, he met a boorish group of city types and spent half of the holiday going off to play golf with them, leaving Kay on her own by the pool with only her Walkman and a bunch of cassettes for company.

"Please, Kay," he whined, tears pouring down his face. "Don't leave me. I've never loved anyone the way I love you."

She could quite easily have cut him to shreds right then. It would have been so easy to humiliate him right in front of everyone at the neighbouring tables, whose attention they were beginning to attract. But she didn't want a scene right now. There would be better opportunities to get her revenge on later trips back to the past. Today, her focus was elsewhere. She just wanted to get away and get on that plane.

"I'm sorry, Alan," she replied. "I'm going and that's that." Without saying any more, she got up, turned around and walked away.

"Don't leave me, Kay!" he shouted behind her. "I'll kill myself if you do."

"Be my guest," she said under her breath. This was getting ridiculous. She had never seen anything so pathetic from a grown man. It had been bad enough the first time around, but at least he had stopped after she had said she would stay. This was downright embarrassing.

"Just keep walking," she kept saying to herself, over and over again, and she did not look back until she had reached passport control.

Chapter Five
June 1995

Only when she was safely in the passport control queue did Kay dare to look behind her. It was a relief when she saw no sign that Alan was following her.

She fumbled in her bag for her passport and had a momentary panic when she thought she couldn't find it. She wouldn't have put it past him to have taken it out of her bag as a backup plan to ensure she couldn't go, but then she realised he couldn't have. She had shown it when she checked in. Then she remembered she had put it in a small, zip-up side pocket of her bag.

Once she was through passport control and security a palpable sense of relief washed over her. She was safe now, wasn't she? She certainly hoped so. She wouldn't put it past him to buy a ticket for the flight, follow her onto the plane, and either beg her to get off or insist on her coming with him.

She had seen similar scenes in films, but she dismissed it as unlikely. Things like that just didn't happen in real life. Besides, he probably didn't even have his passport so it wasn't worth worrying about.

She browsed around the duty-free shops and bought an overpriced sandwich and a drink. Even by 2018 standards, the prices were outrageous. Then she went out into the main departure lounge to see if the gate number for her flight had come up yet.

The airport was still quiet given the early hour, so it was easy for her to get a seat in front of one of the boards giving out flight details. She was not best pleased to discover that her flight was one of a number that had been delayed.

It had been pushing it, aiming to reach Rovaniemi by midnight, even if the flight had been on time. When she had initially planned this trip, back in 1995, she had not intended to do the whole journey in one day at all. She had planned to stay in Helsinki for a day or two and then get an overnight train north, saving the cost of a night in a youth hostel by sleeping on the train. It was a long journey, something she had discovered when she realised that the Scandinavian countries were much larger than she had originally thought.

The capitals of Oslo, Stockholm and Helsinki were more or less on the same latitude, but far further from the Arctic Circle than she had believed. Initially, she had considered travelling to Norway but had been put off when she found out that it was over a thousand miles from Oslo to Tromsø, which was the main city in the north. That was some serious mileage.

She had settled on Rovaniemi as it was a more achievable five hundred miles, but even that was going to take over twelve hours on a train. Under any normal circumstances that wouldn't have mattered, but these were not normal circumstances.

She only had one day, and she wasn't even sure how much of that day she had. Would it end at midnight, whisking her away back to the dismal reality of her flat? Or would she get a full twenty-four hours? She should have asked the angel when she had the chance.

It was clear that with the flight delayed, reaching Rovaniemi in one day wasn't going to be possible by road or rail. But the angel had said it was achievable, and there was one other option open to her.

She reached into her purse where she had a wallet containing her cash and traveller's cheques. The money was meant to last three months, but she didn't need it to last that long anymore. It only had to last a day, so she may as well make use of it.

Because of the cost, she had not originally planned to take any additional air travel other than the Helsinki flight and a flight back from Athens in September. Now things had changed. She could afford to get a domestic flight north once she arrived in Helsinki.

There was no way for her to find out what flights were available at the moment; she would have to wait until she got there. If she had been in the modern world, her smartphone would have been able to give her this information in minutes but she wasn't, so she was just going to have to trust to luck that things worked out for her when she got to Helsinki.

Despite not being able to find out anything about flights she was feeling quite glad that she did not have a mobile phone. It gave her quite a liberating feeling. Not only was she not a slave to Facebook or feeling the temptation to take selfies of everything she was doing, but it also meant she could not be contacted.

That meant she did not have to cope with calls, texts and messages from Alan, pleading pathetically at her not to go. Thankfully she was going to be spared all of that. The less technological past was not a bad place to be right now at all. She was to all intents and purposes incommunicado, and she liked it.

She munched on her cheese and pickle sandwich and watched the board, willing the red DELAYED label to disappear from next to her flight. Once she had finished eating, she passed some time by wandering into the duty-free shop to check out the prices of the alcohol and tobacco.

Although her forty-three-year-old self had taken up smoking in a big way, she had never touched cigarettes as a clean-living teenager. Looking at the incredibly cheap duty-free prices on offer now for boxes of 200, she realised she no longer felt any desire to smoke.

Why was that? she pondered. She was reminded of her libido that morning after she had woken. It seemed that the messages her body was sending to her brain were the genuine physical reactions of her nineteen-year-old self. Yet the cognitive parts of her brain and her memories were very definitely those of her older self.

It was a powerful combination – the unspoiled body of youth with the wisdom and experience of age. Most people never got to experience those things working in tandem. By the time they had gained the latter, the former was gone. But today she had it all and felt like she could conquer the world.

Looking at the cigarettes right now, she felt repulsed and made a mental note that as soon as she got back to 2018 she would do her utmost to stop, even if that old, addicted body's cravings were telling her otherwise. Stopping smoking could be her first step in the right direction. It was unlikely she would have come to this conclusion if she had not come here. The angel had said experiencing the past would help her change the future. Perhaps this was the first example.

Alcohol was another matter. The bottles of half-price spirits were very tempting. She was pleased to see that there were no restrictions on their purchase, recalling that in modern times you couldn't get the duty-free deals if you were travelling within the EU. It seemed that in 1995 these restrictions had not yet been implemented, so she picked herself up a duty-free bottle of vodka. She had no qualms at all about this. Vodka had been her favourite drink since she had started sneaking into The Railway Arms with all the other underage drinkers when she was seventeen.

Maybe she should cut down on her booze, too, but not today. If all went according to plan, she hoped to be celebrating come midnight with a drink in her hand as if it were New Year's Eve. With this in mind, she also picked up a half-bottle of champagne. Why not? It would be extra weight to lug about, and she had no way of chilling it, but if there was ever a special occasion that demanded it, tonight would be it.

Emerging from the duty-free shop, she was delighted to see that the delay was over and her gate was being called.

As she wandered through the airport, it struck her that things had not changed very much in the world of air travel in the past quarter of a century. There was little around her to suggest that she was spending a day in the past.

She had found more signs of change in her handbag than in her surroundings. The lack of a mobile phone was compensated for by other devices that did jobs that her phone did in 2018 – a disposable camera and a cassette Walkman. Looking inside, she found a TDK D90 cassette tape with "Kay Compilation Volume 4" written on it.

Seeing the tape brought a host of memories flooding back. She had spent hours in her teens recording tracks from CDs onto cassettes, trying to create the perfect compilation tape. It was a much more complex process than the modern equivalent of dragging tracks into a playlist.

When making a tape, there was only one real chance to get it right, as they never sounded as good when they had been recorded on more than once. There were all sorts of factors to take into account, the most difficult being to get the songs to fit correctly into the amount of time on the cassette.

Kay always used to try and plan her recordings so that there was no blank space left at the end of the tape. So if she had only five minutes left at the end of one side, it was a case of finding two short tracks or one long one. The worst possible scenario was losing the last few seconds of a song because the tape had run out.

Running order was just as important. It couldn't just be a random collection of favourite tracks. It had to flow, just like a decent album did. And most importantly of all, it had to kick off with a killer track to set the scene.

Putting the headphones to her ears, she pressed play and her eardrums were instantly assailed by the opening bars of "Smells Like Teen Spirit" by Nirvana. She listened for a bit, remembering how much this song had inspired her as a teenager, then switched off as the time had come to board.

She could listen to the rest on the flight, indulging herself in this simple, uncomplicated pleasure. She never seemed to spend any time listening to music anymore. There were simply too many other distractions in the modern world.

She didn't have her tapes anymore either. Alan had taken them all up to the local tip when he was having a clear-out without asking her. When she had protested, he had said they were obsolete. They no longer had a cassette player in the house, so what was the point in keeping them?

He didn't understand that there were memories locked up in those tapes, and all the hours of fun compiling them. Now they were gone forever, buried under a mountain of decomposing chicken bones and babies' nappies.

Boarding went smoothly and in a matter of minutes, she was seated on the plane. The plane was something else that didn't seem to have changed much in the last quarter of a century. It was exactly the same design as pretty much every other plane she had ever been on.

She now had time to relax and listen to her tape. It wasn't a long flight, no more than an hour and a half, which gave her time to ponder what she should do with the remaining five days she had. She had barely had time to take stock of her situation until now, but sitting in her seat, the truth of what she was doing suddenly hit her.

"I am really here! This is really happening," she said out loud, attracting an odd glance from the middle-aged woman in the seat next to her. Kay had a habit of speaking out loud to no one in particular and right now she felt so liberated she wanted to shout out, "I'm free!" at the top of her voice but resisted the temptation to do so. Instead, she sat back quietly and thought carefully about how to make the best of this amazing opportunity she had been given.

She could use her days for pleasure, reliving the highlights of her life in a sort of greatest hits compilation, rather like one of her tapes.

She could go back to pivotal moments like the one she had just experienced in the airport with Alan, and see how things might have turned out differently, for that day at least.

Or she could make a bucket list of things to do, like seeing the midnight sun. The only restriction was she only had one day to make these things happen, but you could do a lot in one day, provided it didn't involve anything on the other side of the world.

There may have been limitations on travel due to time, but there were no such restrictions where money was concerned. Anything expensive could go on a credit card that would never need to be paid off.

Those were all positive ideas, but she had darker thoughts, too, invariably involving Alan. What would it feel like to kill him? She found herself picturing the shocked expression on his face as she plunged a carving knife into his chest. Could she bring herself to do something like that?

No, she couldn't, but she could sure as hell humiliate him in some way. Her mind mused over the possibilities. Jilt him at the altar? Expose his infidelities? All these ideas were satisfying in one way or another, but would they be worth it? Was petty revenge really what she wanted to do with her days? She was better than that, wasn't she? Surely there must be better ways of utilising her time.

There were so many possibilities that she was finding it difficult to narrow them down into anything concrete. The angel had said six days were enough, but were they? Kay could easily have thought of sixty things to do if she had put her mind to it. Perhaps she needed to try and combine some of her ideas in some sort of time-travelling multitasking.

Maybe she could right a wrong, live out a missed experience and make some positive contribution to her future all on the same day if she picked the right day. She had done a pretty good job with it already in the current day. If she could build on that, then she had an interesting few days ahead of her.

She found it frustrating that she couldn't do anything to change history, but she could see the angel's point on that. She knew all about paradoxes from the time travel films she had seen. If she changed the past so she didn't end up in the flat in the chip shop, then she would never have ended up in the depressing mess that had brought the angel to her door in the first place.

Not being able to take anything back into the past or forward into the future was also very restrictive, but that rule only applied to physical things. It didn't apply to her knowledge. She already had the benefit of hindsight when travelling to the past, which allowed her to make the most of her trips back, but could it work the other way?

Was there anything she could find out in the past that she could utilise to make a difference in her present or the future? The angel hadn't said anything about that. As far as Kay was concerned, the future was still a blank page yet to be written and she alone could change it. She couldn't see that the angel could have any objection, having already stated that she had come to help her get out of the rut she was in.

So what could Kay do in the past to help herself? What secrets could she uncover that might enable her to alter her circumstances going forward?

She thought back to some of the great unsolved crimes of the past. What if she could go back to Whitechapel in the 1880s and unmask Jack the Ripper? Even if she could, would anyone in the present believe her? Or would it just be dismissed as another crackpot theory to add to the dozens that had gone before it?

What about financial gain? Could she go back to 1945 and find out where Hitler's legendary gold train ended up at the end of the war? Or indeed if it even existed. It would be a pretty tall order to find all this out in one day in the middle of a war zone.

These were mere flights of fancy and she quickly realised that she could not do either of these things. She could only revisit days within her own lifetime, so anything before the mid-1970s was completely off-limits to her. In fact, anything before about 1990 would be pretty useless when she thought about it. She would not be able to achieve much as a child with little money or freedom.

There were other cases, more recent, that she could potentially investigate, but where would they get her? She thought back over some high-profile cases of the past few decades. There were children who had vanished in mysterious circumstances, never to be seen again. Then there were the high-profile deaths of people in the public eye, many of them murdered with the perpetrators never found. Who were they?

All the details of where and when these incidents had taken place were well documented. It would certainly be possible for her to be at the scene of the crime, particularly those that had taken place in the UK.

But was it really worth it? She could go back to the exact date and time of a major crime and solve it, but what then? Go to the police fifteen years later claiming she knew who had done it, with no physical evidence to back up what she was doing? At best she would not be believed or labelled as a crank. At worst, the real killers could get wind of what she was doing and decide to make her the next target.

And other than the slim prospect of some reward money if anyone did take any notice of her, what was in it for her? No, she was going to have to abandon this line of thinking for the moment. It wasn't going anywhere.

It seemed that she wasn't making much progress with her plans, so she decided to put them on hold for the time being and concentrate on the day at hand. Already the plane was beginning its descent into Helsinki, so she needed to get her act together and sort out the next leg of the journey.

It was gone midday local time when the plane touched down. Clearing passport control was no problem, but when she got to the baggage carousel, there was no sign of any activity. This was going to hold her up further – or was it?

No, it wasn't. As she stood waiting by the stationary carousel, she suddenly realised that she didn't need the rucksack. She reminded herself that she was here for a day, not for the whole three months. So what need did she have to cart around three months of clothes and several heavy guidebooks all day?

All she needed was what was in her handbag and her duty-free bag containing the two bottles she had bought at Heathrow. By the time her rucksack made it onto the carousel, she would be long gone. It could travel round and round to its heart's content. Every time she flew, there always seemed to be one sad little piece of luggage nobody wanted left behind. Today, it might as well be hers.

Leaving the rucksack proved to be a wise choice. She sailed through Customs and back out into the main part of the airport. She headed straight for the check-in desks to investigate the availability of domestic flights.

She was in luck. There was a flight to Rovaniemi at 3.55pm and there were seats available. She had been pretty confident that there would be. After all, the angel had said the trip was achievable, suggesting she must have known about this flight. Kay had plenty of time. So she could have retrieved her rucksack after all, but it didn't matter. She would travel much lighter without it.

Everything went smoothly with the second flight. Just after 6pm, she emerged from Rovaniemi Airport into the bright evening sunshine. She had made it with nearly six hours to spare!

She had expected it to be cold this far north but it was surprisingly warm, like a pleasant early summer's day in England. The sun was low in the sky as if sunset was not far away, but she knew that not to be the case. She remembered from watching a sped-up film on the television that close to the North Pole in summer the sun stayed close to the horizon, doing a complete circle of the skyline over the course of a day.

She took a taxi into the town, wondering how to make the most of the hours ahead. She was very hungry and made finding some food her top priority. She soon found a lovely, old-fashioned-looking café overlooking the river and decided to stop for a bite to eat.

The proprietors did not speak any English and her Finnish dictionary was back in Helsinki in her rucksack. So she took a chance ordering at random from the menu and chose something called lihapullat which turned out to be a delicious dish of traditional Finnish meatballs in gravy.

Later she walked around the town, finding a lively bar packed with young people. Remembering that she was now one of them again, not the middle-aged drunk that the young people of her home town avoided, she ordered a drink and got chatting with a group of young Finnish people.

Unlike the old couple who ran the café, most of these people had a reasonable grasp of English. Perhaps that was a generational thing. She told them all about her trip and asked where the best place was to see the midnight sun. They directed her to a place called Ounasvaara Fell, just outside the town.

Bidding her new friends farewell, she followed their instructions and headed for the fell. It took her nearly an hour to climb to the peak, by which time it was after 11pm. The sun was very close to the horizon now, but it was still broad daylight outside and still warm. She sat herself down at the peak and took in the glorious view of the town below her basking in the late-night sun.

Cracking open her vodka, she took a swig and sat contentedly, just watching the sun as it travelled along the skyline. This had been an amazing day and it had left her feeling fulfilled for the first time in years. It didn't matter that it was only a copy of her universe and that soon she would have to go back to her older self. The point was she was here now and living in a moment that had been taken away from her once before. This time, she was here, and it was happening at last.

As her watch reached midnight, a feeling of euphoria and triumph flooded through her. She uncorked the champagne, and swigged from the bottle like a Grand Prix driver on the top of a podium, even if the bottle didn't quite have the same dimensions as one of Lewis Hamilton's.

She feared that she might be whisked away at that precise moment, back to the flat in 2018, but nothing happened. She continued to watch the sun, swig her champagne and muse about her life. There was no one else up on top of the fell. She was completely alone, enjoying her special moment in this special place. Right then she felt as if the whole world belonged completely to her. In a way, it did, for this world would soon cease to exist, and only she would go on.

Later she felt tired and lay down on the grass to rest. She could quite happily have drifted off to sleep right there and then and never woken up again. It wouldn't have been a bad time to go. The day had given her a sense of completion and at least she would have died happy.

But it wasn't time to go yet. Her trip to the midnight sun had given her plenty to think about. Most importantly, during that last hour, while she was enjoying her champagne, she had worked out exactly where and when she wanted to go next.

Chapter Six
December 2018

Kay wasn't sure how long she had been asleep but suddenly she found herself back in the bathroom, standing in front of the mirror. It was an odd sensation. She didn't feel like she had just woken up and nor did she feel tired. Her return was instantaneous, almost as if she had been placed back into her body exactly when and where she had left it.

"Feels weird, doesn't it?" said the angel. "Most people feel a bit disorientated at first. I call it time travel jetlag. You may have been in the past for a whole day, but here, no time has passed at all."

"That's handy," replied Kay. "As I'm due in work this morning, and I can't afford to lose this job. I don't think they would need much excuse for sacking me, and failing to turn up on the last Saturday before Christmas would see me out on my ear for sure."

"Well, best you get yourself off to work, then," replied the angel.

"What about my next voyage to the past?" asked Kay. "I'm getting a taste for this now."

"I find it works best if I let people have a twenty-four-hour break between trips," replied the angel. "It gives them a chance to reflect on where they've been and plan properly for the next one."

"That seems sensible enough," said Kay. "I've got something in mind, but there's someone I'm hoping to talk to first before I go. What I am planning to do in the past directly involves him."

"There you are, then," said the angel. "Get yourself all prepared then you can make the most of your time when you go back. Before I say goodbye for today, how did you feel your first trip went?"

"It went brilliantly!" exclaimed Kay. "Exactly as I hoped, and I even got to see that ex-worm of my husband snivelling and grovelling like the big baby he is and always was."

"Fantastic," said the angel. "Well, I must pop off and let you get ready for work now. I will see you back here again at the same time tomorrow morning."

As soon as she had spoken, the angel's image was replaced by that of Kay's current self. It wasn't a pretty picture and a solemn reminder that she wasn't the beautiful, young version of herself that she had so enjoyed being again over the previous twenty-four hours.

Not wanting to gaze at her undesirable current appearance any longer than necessary, she hurriedly brushed her remaining teeth and headed back into the bedroom to get dressed. It was still freezing cold. She was going to have to speak to the landlord about it.

That was not a conversation she was looking forward to, but she had no choice. She would freeze to death up here if the weather stayed like it was. There would not be time to track him down this morning. It was five to nine and she needed to rush or she would be late for work.

There was no one in the chip shop downstairs anyway, but there never was at that time in the morning. She let herself out and walked the couple of hundred yards or so to the store as quickly as she dared on the icy ground. She arrived with seconds to spare and headed out the back to put on her overalls. It was going to be a busy day. The shop would be full of mums and dads buying last-minute Christmas presents and she would be rushed off her feet delivering the orders.

Half past five couldn't come soon enough. As soon as the store closed, she was out of the door and heading home. On her way back she psyched herself up ready to confront her landlord about her heating and hot water. She knew from experience it was unlikely to be a cordial conversation.

As soon as she approached the shop doorway, she spotted him. She could hardly miss him, the sweaty mound of middle-aged blubber that he was. Entering the chippy, she could see that he was berating one of the younger members of staff, a friendly, young Eastern European girl called Anna who had served Kay several times in recent weeks.

"Do I make myself clear?" she heard McVie saying in his familiar Scottish twang. "Do I have to get a fucking Polish dictionary and write it down for you? It's two scoops of chips per portion, not three. Are you trying to put me out of business? You'd like that, wouldn't you? Then you can get all your family to come over here and take over my shop, just like your lot are taking over the rest of this country."

The poor girl nodded her understanding, seemingly on the verge of tears. Turning away, McVie caught sight of Kay, who was standing horrified at the racist abuse she had just witnessed. Trying to keep her composure, she spoke quietly.

"Mr McVie, could I have a quick word, please?"

"Well, well, look what the cat's dragged in," replied McVie. "I've been waiting for you. I think it's the other way around, don't you? It's about time I was having some serious words with you. I suggest we go up to the flat."

The thought of having this revolting excuse for a human being up in her flat wasn't a pleasant one, but since she was going to have to show him the malfunctioning heating she didn't have a lot of choice. She unlocked the door and made her way up, hearing his heavy footsteps on the stairs behind her, and his wheezing as he grew short of breath after three or four steps.

"Nice arse," he commented. "Shame about the face. Still, you don't look at the mantelpiece when you're stoking the fire, do you?" He started guffawing loudly as if he had just made the best joke in the world.

70

She had heard both these phrases before, on some ancient sitcom she had watched one night on ITV4. His pathetic attempts at sexist humour belonged in the past, along with his racist remarks to Anna. Ignoring the temptation to say something in retaliation, she tried to take the initiative as he dragged his flabby frame up the stairs and into her room.

"I'll come straight to the point," she said. "My heating and hot water have stopped working."

"I already know," he said, with a grin on his face that she didn't like the look of one bit. "It was me who turned them off."

"Why?" she said. "You can't do that."

"I can do whatever I like if you don't pay the rent," he said. "It was due three days ago, and your direct debit was declined by your bank. Pay up, and I'll turn the heating back on."

"I don't have the money," said Kay, softly. "I haven't been paid yet. You expect a thousand a month for this flat and it's daylight robbery."

"That's the going rate, my love," replied McVie. He was standing uncomfortably close to her and the smell of his body odour mixed in with the all-pervading fishy smell that had permeated his clothes was overpowering. On top of that, there was his breath which was seriously rank.

"Let me tell you," he continued. "There are two types of people in this town these days. Those who own property,

71

like me. And those who don't, like you. It's all a case of supply and demand. If you don't want to pay the market rate, there are plenty of desperate mugs out there that will."

"A thousand pounds might be the going rate for a decent flat, but look at the state of this place. Nothing works properly, you never do any maintenance, and as for health and safety, you must be joking. I'd like to know what the authorities would have to say about it. Where's the smoke alarm? Where's the gas safety certificate?"

She stopped as McVie advanced towards her, a look of pure menace in his eyes. For a moment she feared he was going to attack her.

"Don't try getting clever with me, missy," he said, "or your feet won't touch the floor. You owe me money, and if it's not paid by Christmas Eve then it'll be the electricity I'll be cutting off next. You'll be cooking your turkey by candlelight. If you can even afford one, that is."

"I haven't got it, and you know it," replied Kay. "I don't get paid until next week. I've put a huge amount of overtime in this month, so I'll be more than able to cover it then."

"That's no good to me, love," said McVie. "I've got expenses to pay. I'm planning a big trip up to Scotland next week for Hogmanay and I need some spends."

"Please, Mr McVie," pleaded Kay, despising herself for having to grovel to this disgusting man. "Cut me some slack.

I'll be able to give you 800 quid next week. Maybe I could do a few shifts in the shop downstairs for you to make up the rest."

"Why should I need you to do that?" said McVie. "I've got plenty of migrant workers that are willing to work for under the minimum wage. No questions asked, no tax, no National Insurance." He paused, eyeing up Kay's body. "You know you may be an ugly cow but you haven't got too bad a body for you, considering your age. How old are you? Fifty?"

"I'm forty-three, and what's that got to do with anything?" Kay was incensed at his comments.

He moved closer, invading her personal space once more, forcing her to shrink back towards the bed.

"You know you wouldn't be too bad if it weren't for those teeth. Turn around and show me your arse again," he demanded.

"You can fuck off," replied Kay, finally snapping and raising her voice. "What the fuck do you think I am?"

"Come off it, love, don't be shy. I've seen you bringing all sorts of dodgy fellas up here over the past few months. If you can't pay me the money you owe me, then you can pay me in kind. You might be putting on a bit of weight, but I'm not fussy. You'll do."

"You must be bloody joking!" shouted Kay. He was still moving towards her, a disgusting look of lust in his little piggy eyes that bulged out of his pudgy face. As she backed slowly away, she reached the edge of the bed and now tripped, falling backwards, spreadeagling herself on the mattress.

"Yes, that's the idea, sweetheart. Come on, come to Daddy, you know it makes sense. Two hundred short, you say? Well, let's call that four shags and a blowie between now and when I leave for Scotland next week, plus the 800 quid you've got coming next week and we'll call it quits until next month."

With that, he bellyflopped down onto the bed, trying to pin her down underneath him. Fitter and slimmer than him, she just about managed to wriggle out of his way and jump up. Running across to the window, she wrenched it open, part of the rotting wooden frame coming away in her hand.

"Let's get something clear," she said firmly, trying to disguise the fear in her voice. "No matter how desperate I get, I have no intention of selling myself for money, and especially not to a disgusting pig like you. Now you've got ten seconds to get off that bed and get out that door, or I swear I'll scream rape out of this window."

Kay meant every word and felt strangely euphoric as she said it. Perhaps she had brought some of her youthful fire back from her recent trip to the past. She had not felt this strong and energised for a very long time. Whatever the reason for her newfound bravado, her forceful stance had the desired effect.

Wheezing as he winched his gargantuan frame off the bed, McVie looked furious, but with relief, she saw that he was cooperating. For one horrible moment there she had thought that he was going to force himself upon her.

He walked towards the door, but when he got there he turned back, unable to resist having a final dig.

"You think you're a big, brave lassie, but I can have you anytime I want. Right now, I've got other fish to fry."

Under other circumstances, this might have seemed like a reasonable pun, assuming he was referring to the chip shop, but Kay was in no mood for jokes.

"Just get out," she ordered.

"Don't fret. I'm out of here – for now, but this isn't over. Oh, and I suggest you get yourself a nice, warm jumper because you're going to need it. That heating's staying off and it'll be the electricity next."

With that, he turned on his heels and clumped back down the stairs.

The rush of adrenalin she had felt during the confrontation was now fading, supplanted by relief of the sort that made her burst into tears. Composing herself, she went into the bathroom and did her best to make herself presentable. As she had explained to the angel, there was someone that she was hoping to see tonight and she wanted to make a good impression on him.

She felt hungry, and on any other night would have gone downstairs to get some chips. Despite the scene she had witnessed downstairs earlier, she knew that Anna would give her an extra-large portion of chips. She had formed quite a rapport with the young Polish girl who was one of the few people around who seemed to have any time for Kay these days. But tonight she decided to give it a miss.

Going downstairs could mean running into McVie again, and she didn't want to do anything that would get Anna into trouble. She wouldn't put it past McVie to sexually harass her as well after the conversation earlier. He really was an absolute bastard. Not the same type of bastard as Alan, but a bastard all the same.

She seemed to attract them in all shapes and sizes. Did she have some sort of tracking device buried somewhere inside that enabled them to home in on her? It certainly seemed that way and it had been going on ever since that fateful night of the summer ball when she had taken up with Glen a quarter of a century ago.

But tonight was going to be different because there was one man who she knew was different. His name was Richard Kent, a retired policeman whom she had known since her school days. She had had a crush on him then, and she still had it now, though she had reluctantly accepted that nothing was ever going to come of it. He was married and had firmly rebuffed all her advances towards him.

She hadn't pushed it. She wasn't a homewrecker, despite her recent behaviour and after the experience of having her teeth punched out it would be very foolish of her to make the same mistake again. She had only seen his wife, Debs, a couple of times but those were enough to show Kay that she wasn't someone to get on the wrong side of.

On one of those occasions, just a couple of weeks ago, Debs had made a scene by turning up at the pub one Saturday lunchtime and dragging him out over some unfulfilled promise to take her Christmas shopping. Another time, he had stayed in the pub so long one afternoon that she had brought his Sunday dinner down to the pub and slapped it down on the bar in front of him.

No, Mrs Kent was not a woman to be trifled with. But that was OK because nothing was going to happen between Kay and her husband – at least not in this place and at this time. But what Kay had in mind would be taking place in the past before Kent had even met his wife. Not only that, it would not even be in the same universe.

A few weeks ago, Kay and Kent had got talking in the pub. He was in there a lot these days since he had lost his job, and they had rekindled their friendship that dated back to schooldays.

That night they had a heart-to-heart conversation about the end-of-term ball and the turn of events that had led to her ending up in the disastrous relationship with Glen. Emboldened by alcohol, she had worn her heart on her sleeve and told him everything.

When she revealed how Glen had manipulated her into being his ball date and explained how deep down she had wanted to go with Kent instead, she could see that she had caught his attention.

Since that conversation, she had noticed a distinct change in the way he was around her. Before he had clearly found her attentions irritating towards her, but his attitude had now softened considerably. She knew this wasn't in an amorous or lustful way: he had made that quite clear. What he had done was go out of his way to be friendly towards her, asking her how she was getting on and offering her advice on her troubles.

Perhaps he felt sorry for her and was trying to make up for her disappointment in the past. Whatever the reason, something had changed between them, and it was a welcome change. Apart from him and Anna, she couldn't think of a single other person she could even begin to class as a friend. She had plenty of other acquaintances in the pub, but they weren't real friends, just fellow drinkers down on their luck normalising each other's behaviour as they drowned their sorrows together.

During her boring day lugging packages out of the stockroom at work, she had been given plenty of time to work out a plan for her next trip back in time. Ever since that conversation with Kent in the pub, her thoughts had frequently drifted back to that ball and how things might have turned out differently.

That night with Glen had been the point when the seeds of her problem had been sown. She had lost her virginity to him that very night, underneath the slide in one of the kids' playgrounds on the new estate. It had all been very undignified and unsatisfactory. She had accepted it at the time as most girls said the first time wasn't anything to write home about, but with Glen, things didn't improve with practice.

She didn't know much better at the time, having no one else to compare him to, but she suspected things were not quite right. Sex with him certainly wasn't the mind-blowing experience that the articles in her *More!* magazines suggested it should be.

How different might that first time have been if it had been Kent who had taken her home that night? Well, she was going to do her utmost to find out. But before she did, she wanted the chance to talk to his present self again about the events of that day. In particular, she wanted to ensure that he would have gone with her given the opportunity. From what he had said before, she was pretty sure he would have.

She cleaned herself up as best she could with no hot water available, put on some lipstick and tried to make her hair semi-presentable. It wasn't perfect but it would have to do. Ignoring the rumblings in her stomach, she rushed through the chip shop, managing to avoid being spotted by McVie who was busy counting the money in the till. Then she was out through the door, heading for The Red Lion on another chilly December night.

79

Chapter Seven
December 2018

It was busy when she got to The Red Lion, but not so much as the previous night when the dance floor area at the top had been so rammed that she had struggled to fight her way through to the toilets.

Down at the front of the pub, where the older regulars gathered, she could see the usual suspects at the bar. Kent was there, deep in discussion with a couple of others. Further up the pub, on the right-hand side, she could see a bunch of teenagers who were often in the pub playing pool. To the left of them, the dance floor area was pretty quiet but it was only half past seven. The disco wouldn't be starting for over an hour yet.

Sidling up to the bar, she picked up the gist of the conversation that was going on. Andy, one of the pub's regular alcoholics was talking about the news story that had been on everyone's lips the past few days – the double murders in Oxford and Kidlington.

"Where's Inspector Morse when you need him, eh?" remarked Andy, before lifting his freshly poured pint to his mouth to take a swig of lager. He didn't quite hit the target, which was surprising because it wasn't as if he hadn't had enough practice. As a consequence, a few drips dribbled down his chin and onto the ancient denim jacket that he always wore. Kay wondered how many he had had today. She knew he started at lunchtime most days and had clearly been on a mission judging by the wet patches down both the jacket and his matching jeans.

"I'm sure the police are on the case," replied Kent.

Kay knew all about the murders. There was a radio in the back of the warehouse at work. It was tuned into the local radio station and she had heard updates on the hourly news bulletins, in between the bland, predictable playlist and amateurish adverts for local businesses.

The first murder had taken place six days ago in the Summertown area of Oxford, followed four days later by a second in Kidlington. It hadn't taken a genius to work out that the murders were connected. Both the victims were young, Eastern European women, and both had been raped and then knifed to death. The whole grisly affair had shocked the community, and the press had been all over it. It hadn't taken them long to come up with a nickname for the suspect once the connection between the two murders had been revealed – the somewhat unimaginative "Christmas Killer".

"You were the police until not long ago," said Andy to Kent. "What would you have done?"

"Well, we would have made door-to-door enquiries, taken forensic evidence from the scene..." began Kent, before Andy interrupted, not interested in the content of Kent's answer, only in dismissing it.

"So bugger all, then," said Andy. "Well, I just hope the Oxford police do a better job of it than you would have. Good

81

job these murders weren't in this town – the residents would be scared shitless if you were still in charge."

Ever since Kent had lost his job, Andy had been sticking the boot in. Kay thought he could do with some moral support.

"That's a bit harsh, Andy," said Kay, seizing her chance to enter the conversation. "I thought he was the best head of local police we ever had."

Andy looked up, registering her presence for the first time through his booze-laden eyes. "Oh, it's you. Well, you would say that wouldn't you? Everyone knows you're desperate to shag him. Though God knows why: I doubt whether he's even up to it, look at the size of him. I doubt whether he can even find it these days."

"Actually, I've lost a bit of weight recently," said Kent defensively. "I'm under eighteen stone now."

"I thought so," said Kay, looking at him closely. He was definitely looking slightly less flabby and a little more toned. "Have you joined a gym?"

"I just had a bit of a re-evaluation of my life recently," he replied. "After I lost my job it would have been easy to let myself slide into middle-aged sloth and eaten and drunk myself into an early grave. I guess I just realised I'm only forty-two, and I've plenty to live for. So I've started exercising and cut down on the post-pub food."

"You say that, but you're still knocking back the booze," commented Andy.

He really was an irritating pain in the arse, thought Kay, constantly interrupting other people's conversations. She was not going to be able to have the discussion she wanted to have with Kent while Andy was there, interjecting his snide remarks at every opportunity.

She would have to get him away from the bar. Andy wouldn't follow them: once he got on his bar stool he was practically superglued to it for the night. But first, she needed a drink. In the few minutes since she had entered the pub, it had started to get very busy and, distracted by the conversation, she had taken her attention away from the bar. She seriously had to get that first drink of the day inside her.

There seemed to be only two barmaids on duty and they were buzzing around at a serious rate of knots trying to keep up with the sudden influx of customers. Some were waving notes across the bar in impatient attempts to catch the bar staff's attention. That wouldn't work, thought Kay. In her experience bar staff hated that.

She would have to face the bar and try and catch someone's eye if she was ever to get a drink this evening. She turned away from Andy and Kent temporarily and concentrated on the business at hand, eavesdropping as they continued their conversation.

"You can hardly talk," Kent was saying. "If I was going to put a bet on anyone in this pub drinking themselves to death, you'd be an odds-on favourite."

"I'd die happy, though," said Andy. "Anyway, stop changing the subject. I want the inside info on these murders. Are the police anywhere near catching him?"

"I don't know why you think I'm privy to that knowledge, Andy," replied Kent. "As you so gleefully point out at every opportunity, the police have decided to dispense with my services. Much as I'd appreciate the extra cash, sadly they have not been on the phone begging me to come back to help them crack this case."

"Now there's a surprise," remarked Andy sarcastically. "But still, you must still be in touch with your old colleagues. What about that new D.I. Benson? You could ask her, couldn't you?"

"Why would I want to?" asked Kent. "It's not something desperately eating away at my soul. Besides, it's not on her patch. She's responsible for this town, not what goes on in Oxford and Kidlington. She probably knows no more than I do."

"Which is nothing, by the sound of it," said Andy. "I don't like her anyway. She tried to do me for dropping a fag end outside the pub a while back. Didn't make it stick, though, did she? I was too clever for her."

As was so frequently the case, Kent was becoming irritated by Andy's endless piss-taking so he decided it was time to put the boot on the other foot.

"Why are you so interested anyway? Anyone would think you had something to hide. Have you?"

"I'm not the murderer if that's what you're implying," answered Andy defensively. "Anyway, I've got an alibi. I was in here when both of them took place."

"Wow, really? I never would have guessed," said Kent, turning Andy's earlier sarcasm back at him. "Do you ever go anywhere else?"

Kay had finally managed to catch the eye of one of the barmaids, a young, punky-looking girl with dyed pink hair. Taking hold of her first drink of the night, she lifted it to her lips and took a large, glorious swig of vodka and Coke. She immediately felt better as the strong alcohol slipped down her throat. It was time to get on with what she had come here to do.

She had heard every word of the conversation between Kent and Andy. Despite having her eyes firmly fixed forward towards the bar, rather than on them, it hadn't been difficult to pick up on Kent's irritation with Andy. Turning back towards him, she could see from the annoyed look on his face that he had had enough, so now seemed a good time to intervene.

Catching his eye, she spoke. "Richard, can we talk in private for a minute?"

He looked a little startled by this. Perhaps it was because she had used his first name. Everyone else just called him Kent. And he wasn't the only one to notice this.

"There you go, I knew it!" exclaimed Andy. "First-name terms! I knew there was something going on between you two!"

He turned to the bar, seeking confirmation from the landlord, who had just appeared, called downstairs by one of the stressed barmaids to help man the pumps. "Didn't I say so, Craig?"

"Did you?" said Craig. "I don't remember that. But then, quite honestly, most of what you say goes in one ear and out the other these days. It kind of gets a bit repetitive after a while."

"I bet you a tenner they were having an affair," replied Andy. "Come on, pay up."

"I don't remember that, either," said Craig.

"You must do," protested Andy. "Nobby was here when we made the bet, he'll back me up."

"Well, he's not here, now, is he?" replied Craig.

"He's gone to Towcester Dogs, tonight," said Andy. "He's got a dead cert running there. He got it off that bloke who sells those dodgy TV boxes at Finmere market."

"That sounds like a reliable source," replied Craig. "What could possibly go wrong?"

As they continued their argument, Andy's attention was drawn away from Kay and Kent, who hadn't said anything for the past couple of minutes. He was just standing there with a resigned look on his face, shaking his head slightly at the usual pointless banter going on all around him.

Kay glanced towards the front window of the pub where there was a small table with two chairs free. Two teenage girls were getting up from the table, draining the last of their drinks and putting on their coats. The table wouldn't last long, not on a Saturday. She needed to make a beeline for it before anyone else grabbed it.

"Just ignore them," said Kay. "Come on, Richard, come over here for a minute. I want to ask your advice on something."

She saw him looking at her and hoped that he would take her seriously. She wasn't drunk yet, after all, and hadn't acted like the desperate, middle-aged tart she had probably come across as in the recent past.

"Come on, then," he agreed. "I could do with a break from this idiot."

They managed to get away from Andy unnoticed, as he was still trying to wheedle money out of Craig. Their getaway was timely, as the punky barmaid had decided enough was enough and had intervened between Craig and Andy, desperate to try and get Craig to serve some customers. Kay had noticed that the landlord didn't seem to be that bothered with doing much in the way of work recently. His heart didn't seem to be in the place anymore.

They made it to the table, just before a couple of fat blokes in Oxford United shirts bagged it and sat down.

"What's all this about, Kay?" asked Kent, looking a little wary. "I don't want those two up there gossiping about us. If it gets back to Debs it'll be my chestnuts roasting on an open fire this Christmas."

"Relax," replied Kay. "I'm not after your body. Well, not in this universe anyway."

Kent noticeably perked up at this. "What do you mean by that?" he asked. She had clearly caught his attention.

"Well, the thing is," she began. "I've been thinking about that conversation we had a few weeks ago about the end-of-term ball. Do you remember? When I told you how Glen tricked me into letting him take me to the ball instead of you?"

"Yes," replied Kent, leaning forward intently. "Go on."

"Well, I know it was all a long time ago," she said. "But you must remember that night."

"As it happens, I remember it better than you can possibly imagine," said Kent. "But perhaps not in the same way that you do," he added cryptically.

Now it was Kay's interest that was piqued. What did he mean by that? she wondered. It was an odd remark, but she decided to put it to one side for the moment and press on with what she wanted to say.

"Well, have you ever considered how different our lives might have been if things had taken another path?" she asked. "What would have happened if you had taken me to the ball instead of Glen?"

Now he was looking extremely interested. He looked her intently in the eye and paused to consider his words before he spoke again.

"I have thought about it a great deal, as it happens," he replied. "More than you can know. But what I'm more interested in right now is your sudden interest in the subject – in particular, why?"

She hadn't expected him to show this much interest. Encouraged by it, she continued, eager to see what his response would be to her next question.

"Well, let's just say, for argument's sake, that I could go back in time to that day, ditch Glen and go to the ball with you instead. Do you think we would have got it together? I don't just mean on that night, but afterwards, too. Like boyfriend and girlfriend? I know if you had wanted to, I wouldn't have said no."

"I can't believe you're asking me this," said Kent, the look on his face now bordering on the incredulous. "It's just too big a coincidence."

"What is?" asked Kay.

"What you are talking about doing – going back in time. What put that thought in your head? Or should I perhaps say who? Someone who may have offered you a chance to go back? Someone like a friendly angel, perhaps?"

Kay couldn't believe what she was hearing.

"How could you possibly know that?" she asked.

"Because I've met him, too," replied Kent.

Chapter Eight
December 2018

"Him?" asked Kay. "Don't you mean her?"

"Of course," said Kent. "He would be a she in your case. If it's anything like what happened to me, he, or rather she, will appear as a younger version of you."

"Yes," said Kay, overjoyed to hear that she wasn't the only one. "That's exactly what happened. I have met her and she looks like I was when I was about nineteen. She's offered me the chance to go back in time and relive some past days. I've been back once already."

Over the next few minutes, Kay excitedly poured out everything that had happened so far. When she had finished, Kent confirmed that he, too, had met the angel, been given the same offer, and already completed his six trips back through time. He was just as excited as she was to find another time traveller and was now eager to share some of his experiences with her.

"I'm so glad to find out I'm not alone with all of this anymore," he said. "I didn't feel able to speak to anyone else about this, either when it was happening, or since. How could I have done? People would have thought I was going mad."

"That's what I thought, too. But it's alright now," said Kay. "We can talk to each other. You must tell me all about it. How long ago did it happen?"

"It was only about a month ago," said Kent. "It started the day I lost my job. I was feeling pretty suicidal at the time and couldn't see the point of carrying on. I was up on the roof of Sainsbury's car park and thinking about jumping off. Then the angel just appeared out of nowhere. I didn't even recognise myself at first. Funny, isn't it? You don't notice your body changing from day to day, but when you look at yourself twenty-five years ago it's quite a shock to see how much age has taken its toll."

"Tell me about it," said Kay, understanding exactly what he meant after comparing the vision of loveliness that was her earlier self with her ragged current appearance. "So let's hear some more about your trips. How did you decide what days to go back to? I'm still trying to figure out what to do with mine."

Kent related a few tales from his trips back through time, making Kay chuckle with the story of how he had stuck the head of a large, plastic dinosaur up his evil boss's arse.

"I would have loved to have seen that," she said, thoughts of Alan and McVie suddenly springing to mind. "I can think of one or two people I wouldn't mind doing something similar to myself."

Her mind was opening up to all manner of possibilities. Discovering that she had a kindred spirit in Kent had been a welcome and unexpected development. The yearning she felt towards him was stronger than ever, but it was more than that now. There was a new and unique bond between them. He was her co-conspirator, and her partner in time. She intended to make the most of it.

Kay decided it was time she brought the subject back around to the day of the ball since that was what she had originally come to talk to him about.

"So, in terms of which days to choose, I'm seriously considering going back to live the day of the ball over again. The reason I want to ask you about this is that it directly concerns you. I want to see if I can change things on the day so that it is you who takes me to the ball rather than Glen. How would you feel about that?"

Kent paused, clearly deep in thought about how he should respond.

"OK, I'll be honest with you," he said. "I've already been there. Just like you, I wondered how that day might have turned out differently, so it was one of the days I chose."

"What happened?" asked Kay, eager to hear more.

"I'm not sure I should say," he said. "I don't think I ought to influence what you do when you go back there. You should follow your own path."

"But you already know how it all turned out," she said. "At least you can tell me if it's worth my while going back

93

there. If you don't want to take me to the ball, or you didn't want to back then, then I'd be wasting my time."

"I did want to take you to the ball," replied Kent. "That's not exactly what I meant, though. You see, I know how it turned out for me when I went back. But remember, you'll be going back to a completely new version of that day, not the one that I went back to."

Kay nodded, remembering what the angel had said. "I see what you mean," she said. "The angel creates a copy each time she sends us back. In effect, this will be a third version of the day, different both from the original and from the one you experienced on your trip."

"That's exactly right," said Kent. "As soon as you get there, things will start to deviate from what happened on my visit because it will be you changing things this time, rather than me."

"It's very complicated, all of this," replied Kay. "So, just to clarify, I will be starting the day with a clean sheet of paper. That means it doesn't matter if you tell me what you did on your trip because it won't be that version of you that I encounter."

"You're right, it won't be that version," said Kent. "At no point are we going to meet up in the past both remembering all of this. When you get there, you will meet my blissfully unaware seventeen-year-old self who will know nothing about any of this. That gives you a significant advantage over me, and everyone else, come to that."

"It's not like you didn't have that advantage when you went back, though, was it?" asked Kay. "And knowing how I felt about you…how I still feel about you, it wouldn't have been difficult for you to take advantage of me. Not that I would have minded, obviously."

"I hardly think I was taking advantage of you," said Kent. "From what I recall it was you coming on to me."

"So something did happen then?" exclaimed Kay, enthusiastically.

"Look, you've wheedled enough information out of me already," said Kent. "We probably shouldn't even be having this conversation – it might contravene the angel's rules, not that he's particularly forthcoming on that front. All I'm willing to say at this stage is that I went back there to fix things so that I would be your ball date, rather than Glen. What happened after that I want to keep to myself, at least until you return. Just follow your feelings, enjoy the moment and let things happen naturally."

"That's good enough for me," she said. "By the way, how did you get rid of Glen?"

"Let's just say he was indisposed and leave it at that," replied Kent. "Don't worry: I didn't bump him off or anything."

"I'll need to get rid of him as well," said Kay. "Any suggestions?"

"I'm sure you'll think of something," replied Kent. "He's not as clever as he thinks he is, and you've got all that life experience that he won't have back then."

"You're right, he was all brawn and no brains," said Kay. "I'll get him out of the picture, no problem."

"Right, that's all I'm telling you – for now, at least," said Kent. "We'll compare notes when you come back."

"Thank you," replied Kay, gratefully. "Will you be in here again tomorrow night? I'm meeting the angel again in the morning, and that's when I'm planning to make the trip."

"I wasn't planning on coming down here tomorrow," replied Kent. "Debs doesn't like me going out on Sunday nights. But I am keen to hear how you got on, so I shall try and find a reason to pop down for a bit. And now we really should be getting back to the bar before Andy tells the whole pub we are having an affair."

He drained the last of his pint and got up from the chair, eager to replenish his glass.

"I've often imagined what it would be like if we were," said Kay, instantly regretting it when she saw the irritated look that crossed Kent's face.

"Look, Kay, we need to get one thing clear. Whatever might happen in the trip you are about to take to the past, it's not going to change anything here. I'm happy to be your friend, especially now we've discovered what we have in common, but you must stop thinking we might get together in the future."

"I know," she said. "I'm sorry. I just keep thinking about how different our lives might have been if it hadn't been for Glen wrecking our chance all those years ago."

"Look, just go to the day of the ball and enjoy whatever happens. That's all you can do. Seize the moment."

Kay agreed and the two of them returned to the bar. They had nothing to worry about where Andy was concerned. He was still perched on his stool, now boring a couple of young women who were waiting to get served with his usual fabricated tales about his non-existent rockstar past.

Kay didn't linger in the pub for once, wanting to get a decent night's sleep. She also didn't feel like getting out of her skull to drown her sorrows, as for once she didn't have any. Instead of needing to blot out the misery of her seemingly futile existence, there was suddenly plenty to feel enthusiastic about. She was going on a series of adventures through her own past and life seemed full of possibilities again.

She still felt sad that her crush on Kent seemed destined to remain unrequited, but she had to be realistic and do the right thing. She had vowed she wouldn't mess around with married men: his wife didn't deserve it, and neither did his kids. It was time to accept that they had no future together.

But she had a chance to get this particular monkey off her back in the past. He had more or less given her the green light to go ahead and make the most of the opportunity, and she planned to wring every drop of enjoyment from it that she could.

She was relieved on returning to the chip shop to see there was no sign of the dreaded McVie. She was still hungry so she got herself a bag of chips. She fancied some fish, too, but didn't have enough money for cod. A fresh batch of fish cakes had just been put out, so she ordered one of those instead, before going up to her room to think about the day ahead.

After she had eaten her supper she got into bed and wrapped the duvet around herself. It was still desperately cold in the room.

She flicked on the TV to see if there was anything interesting on, but there was only *Match of the Day* on BBC1. She wasn't interested in football, so flicked across to BBC2 which was showing a rerun of an old panel game. She watched that for a while but it wasn't long before she fell asleep, the TV still playing in the background.

In the morning, she woke refreshed, and even more excited than she had been the night before. She practically bounded out of bed, so keen was she to get started. It was nearly nine o'clock and when she headed into the bathroom, the angel was already waiting for her in the mirror.

"Morning!" said Kay, full of the joys of spring even though her feet were like blocks of ice and the mirror had steamed up as soon as she breathed on it. "And what a fantastic one it's going to be."

The angel's face was a little blurred through the mist, but she could still make out that it had a disapproving look.

"Yes, well, before we get started, we need to get something clear."

"What's that?" asked Kay.

"Confidentiality," replied the angel. "When I gave you this opportunity, I hadn't expected you to go straight down to the pub and start blabbing about it to all and sundry."

"It was hardly all and sundry," protested Kay. "I only told one person and as it turns out, he knows all about you already."

"I know," said the angel. "But I would prefer it if you didn't tell anyone else about any of this. I offer these trips only to a very few selected individuals in the strictest confidence. If everyone started going around telling people about it, where would we be? There would be busloads of time travel tourists, ghost hunters and all sorts of other weirdos turning up here. I'd be bracketed with the Loch Ness Monster and Bigfoot. Everyone would be trying to get a glimpse of me."

"I can't believe you are worried about something like that, what with all the powers you claim to have," replied Kay. "What are they going to do, throw a net over the mirror? Anyway, you never said anything about not telling anyone."

"No, I didn't. Perhaps I should have done," said the angel. "I think it's about time I started issuing a list of terms and conditions to people before I let them loose in the past. Something to make sure they are crystal-clear on the rules before we start."

"Maybe you should," said Kay. "So you don't have to tick me off again, is there anything else I should or shouldn't be doing before we carry on?"

"Just don't tell anyone else," said the angel. "And we will see how we get on."

"Fair enough," replied Kay. "So can we get started now?" she added impatiently.

"We can," said the angel. "This is the bit where I normally ask people where they want to go, but there won't be any prizes for guessing in this case. Would it be the day of the ball, by any chance? It's all you've been thinking about for the past day."

"Got it in one," replied Kay.

"This should be interesting," said the angel. "Often I say when people go back that this will be version 2.0 of the day, but in this case, it's going to be version 3.0. But then you already figured that out, judging by your conversation with Kent last night."

"You know it's quite rude to eavesdrop on private conversations," said Kay, feeling slightly uncomfortable at the thought of the angel monitoring her every move.

"Sorry, it's just that I find this whole process so fascinating, I don't like to miss a single thing that happens," replied the angel. "Don't worry about it. Just go back and enjoy your day."

"And can I talk to Richard about it afterwards?" she asked.

"Well, I can't see in this instance it will matter much," said the angel. "But like I said before, no one else."

"I'm hardly likely to," said Kay. "I don't want to get carted off to the loony bin. Forget coachloads of time travel tourists and the Loch Ness Monster. I'm more likely to end up in a mental institution if I go around telling people I'm a time traveller who talks to an angel in a mirror."

"But you people watch enough movies and films with similarly preposterous premises," said the angel.

"But that's just fantasy," replied Kay. "People watching know it's only a fantasy. If you ask me, the characters in these films are far too accepting of the situation when someone claims to be a time traveller. In real life, if anyone went around claiming to be a time traveller, 99% of people would think they were insane. And the 1% who did believe them would probably be insane themselves. The only reason I believe in it now is because I've seen it with my own eyes. Now can we please have less talk and more action? I've got a ball to go to!"

"Your wish is my command," replied the angel, clicking her fingers in the mirror to bring the conversation to an end.

The next thing she knew, Kay was waking up in her teenage bedroom.

Chapter Nine
July 1994

The sun was pouring through the window and the room was warm. She had travelled back once again to a day in the summer. It was a hot July morning and just like before she felt the energy of youth coursing through her veins.

She sat up and looked around, images of her teenage life all around her. Her duvet cover was bright red and covered in white hearts. The walls were adorned with posters of the indie bands that she had loved in her youth: Saint Etienne, Blur and The Charlatans.

The poster of Saint Etienne's *Foxbase Alpha* album cover triggered some happy memories. They had been the first band she had ever gone to see, a gig at the Equinox Club in Leicester Square in 1993. It had been an amazing night, travelling down with three girlfriends on the train from Oxford. It was one of the most fondly remembered nights of her youth and one she would certainly consider revisiting. She had been at that age when fresh and new experiences were happening all the time.

It was the first and only time she had got to see Saint Etienne live. Years later she found out the band were doing a special 25th anniversary tour celebrating the release of *Foxbase Alpha*. She had wanted to go, but it hadn't happened. She hadn't kept in touch with those two friends. They were long lost in the past.

When she had tentatively mentioned going to one of the reunion concerts to Alan, he dismissed the suggestion as ridiculous. She was far too old to be running around going to gigs, he had said.

That had been pretty much the sort of response she got to most suggestions throughout their relationship. Even when they were younger, he wasn't interested in going anywhere or doing anything remotely exciting.

One year, when her daughter was still a toddler, she had had the chance to go to Glastonbury, but he had put a stop to that, too. He said it was inappropriate for her to go off to a pop festival like that when she had the responsibility of looking after a child, and besides, his golf society was away on one of their trips that weekend. That was the sort of selfish bastard he was.

She needed to forget about Alan for the moment. There would be plenty of time to think up a way for him to get his comeuppance later on. Today was all about her and Kent.

The clock told her it was nearly 8.30am. She wandered across the room to her Sanyo stereo system. It was black ash and had four layers to it. There was a turntable on the top, with a radio on the second layer. The third deck was a CD player and finally a twin cassette deck. She pressed eject on the CD to see what popped out – unsurprisingly, it was *Foxbase Alpha*. Resisting the temptation to listen, instead, she flicked on the radio, keen to immerse herself in the day at hand.

She was greeted by the familiar voice of Steve Wright presenting the breakfast show on Radio 1, along with his posse. It cut to the news which she listened to with interest. The lead story was about O.J. Simpson being tried for murder. She had forgotten all about that, but it had been huge at the time.

The weather forecast said it was going to be hot and sunny with a maximum temperature of 29 °C. She didn't need the radio to tell her that, she could see it was a glorious day just from looking out of the window. In her memories, the ball had taken place on a lovely warm summer evening. Those memories hadn't lied.

She couldn't have asked for better weather. What a tonic after struggling through the cold, dark December days of 2018.

It was time to think more about the day ahead. What were her objectives and how was she going to accomplish them? What did she want to get out of this day?

She was pretty clear what her objectives were. It was how she was going to go about it that was less clear. She needed to bin Glen off and ensure Kent took her to the ball instead. That was the first part, but she wanted more. Kent had told her to seize the moment and that was exactly what she intended to do.

This had been the night she had lost her virginity. She had every intention of seeing that part of history fulfilled, albeit with a different partner. She had to accept that Kent didn't want her in 2018, so this was going to be her one and only chance to sleep with him. It was vital she didn't waste it.

She did not want to waste the rest of the day either. The ball might not be until the evening, but she certainly wasn't going to sit around the house waiting until it was time to go out. She wanted to see as much of Kent as she could, so she needed to get out there and make things happen.

So, she was pretty clear on what she needed to do, but what about the application? How was she going to get rid of Glen? She had enjoyed Kent's tale of how he had spiked him with laxatives. It would have been fun to humiliate him with some similarly diabolical scheme, but time was of the essence. She didn't have time to hatch some elaborate plot. She needed to get the job done quickly and effectively.

All she had to do was tell Glen straight that she wasn't going to the ball with him. It was her prerogative after all. And she wouldn't pull any punches while she was doing it. Glen may have been an arrogant son of a bitch even back then, but he would be no match for Kay with all her years of experience behind her, not to mention the benefit of her hindsight.

She would go and let him know in no uncertain terms what she thought of him. That would be satisfaction enough. As soon as she had done that, she would be straight round to Kent to give him the good news that he did have a date for the ball after all.

She needed to get herself ready. She looked through her wardrobe, delighted to find some long-forgotten favourite clothes that she would never have squeezed her forty-three-year-old frame into. She also found a Catwoman costume hanging there. Of course, she recalled. The theme of the ball had been superheroes.

She picked out a skimpy, pale lemon dress, the perfect item for this gorgeous summer's day. It looked impossibly small but she knew at this age it would fit her.

She dressed quickly, eager to get on with the matter at hand. Going downstairs in search of breakfast, she discovered that the house was empty. Her mum and dad were both out at work. She was initially disappointed, as she very much wanted to see them both again, but consoled herself with the thought that she was sure to see them in the evening.

She hadn't come back to this day purely to relive the ball. Part of her multitasking agenda involved seeing her parents again, which was just as important as seeing Kent, because by 2018 both of them were dead.

Keen to keep her strength up for the day ahead, she prepared herself a decent breakfast of Weetabix and toast, washed down with coffee and orange juice. As she ate alone in the kitchen where she had eaten almost all her meals for the first nineteen years of her life, she sat and thought about her parents.

Kay had been an only child, born to them when they were both over forty. After years of trying and failing to conceive, her mother's pregnancy had come as a complete surprise when it finally happened. By her teenage years, they were already in their late fifties. Both drank an awful lot of alcohol, a trait it seemed Kay had inherited as she grew older. In the end, the drink had killed them both.

Despite being an only child, she had inherited nothing. If she had, she wouldn't be in the mess she was in now. Sadly, her parents had never owned their own home. When they had married in 1963 they had got a council house, as millions of others had in those days. Her dad was a manual worker on the railways and her mother stayed at home. They had never been short of money and had a comfortable living but they had no assets.

Her father had talked about buying the house during the right-to-buy bonanza of the late-1980s, but by then it was too late. Even at the knock-down prices the houses were being offered at, they couldn't get a mortgage. Not only was he considered to be too old, but he had also been forced to retire early through ill health.

She didn't blame her parents for any of this. They had loved her and nurtured her, and that was worth more than any inheritance. But how she wished they were still around in 2018 to give her some sanctuary in the desperate times she had found herself. The day she had left home to live with Alan, her father had promised that there would always be a place for her as long as they were alive.

But they were long gone and she was on her own. Maybe it was for the best. At least they had been spared seeing her in the mess she had ended up in. Her father would probably be turning in his grave if he could see her now, and who could blame him? She felt utterly ashamed at the failure her life had turned out to be. It was one of the things that gnawed away at her every day, driving her to drink.

At least she would see them later, and this would not be the final time either. She would make sure to go back and spend a quality day with them before all of this was over. As for now, it was time to go around and give Glen what was coming to him. She had been looking forward to this.

Heading outside, she made her way down the front path towards the gate, relishing the feel of the warm sunshine on her skin. The signs of summer were everywhere. She could hear the low drone of a light aircraft somewhere overhead, as well as the sound of the next-door neighbour's lawnmower. The lawn in her front garden looked immaculate. She remembered how proud her father had always been of the garden, particularly the year he had won a prize in the Britain in Bloom competition.

The lawn was framed with flower beds containing a colourful variety of flowers. Dozens of bees were buzzing around the buddleia flowers, and there were plenty of butterflies around, too. She watched, amused, as two cabbage whites had a brief coupling in mid-air.

Oh to be as carefree as those butterflies, she thought. They didn't have the stress of mortgages and affairs and divorce settlements. They just got on with it. Still, being an insect, they couldn't afford not to. How long did a butterfly live – one summer, maybe? They certainly didn't have time to waste worrying about their pension plans.

But today, Kay could be as carefree as those butterflies. She could live this day as if she were a mayfly if she wanted to, as a twenty-four-hour life was all she had in this place and time. Quickening her stride, she closed the gate behind her and set off down the street towards Glen's house at a lightning pace.

She didn't have any problem remembering exactly where to go. During their brief relationship, she had been to his house many times, mostly for sex. Glen hadn't been that interested in doing anything else with her. Well, he wasn't going to be getting any today. That was for certain.

His house was at the rougher end of the council estate, next door to a house where an old man in a string vest did up old bangers on his front lawn. She rang the front doorbell and waited, as a dog in a house nearby barked relentlessly.

It seemed to take an age for him to answer the door, and when he did, he looked half-awake and dishevelled in just a T-shirt and boxers. Despite that, it didn't take long for his familiar swagger to manifest itself.

"Kay!" he exclaimed. "I hadn't expected to see you this early. Can't wait to get your hands on me, eh?"

That was exactly how she remembered Glen, cocky and arrogant. "Not exactly," she replied, waiting to see what else he would have to say for himself.

"I was still in bed when you rang the bell," he said. "Getting plenty of shut-eye, you know, to recharge the batteries ready for later. I've got a feeling I'm not going to get much sleep, tonight, what do you reckon?"

He winked at her as he said this like some seedy character out of an ancient *Carry On* film.

"Well, this won't take long," replied Kay, ignoring his corny attempts at humour. "Then you can get back to bed."

"Speaking of which, why don't you join me?" asked Glen. "No need to wait until tonight, is there? I know you're gagging for it: you wouldn't have worn that dress if you weren't."

His eyes were all over her lemon-clad body. He was practically drooling.

"That's what you think, is it?" said Kay. "Oh, by the way, my eyes are on my face, not on my chest. I'd appreciate it if you looked at me properly when I'm speaking to you."

She had a stony look on her face which Glen, tearing his eyes reluctantly away from her breasts, picked up on. His swagger and cockiness began to dissipate as he detected that this hottie on his doorstep wasn't giving off the sorts of signals that suggested she was about to leap into the sack with him.

"Why have you come round, Kay?" he asked, the wind taken out of his sails.

"Just one question," she replied. "Why did you tell me Richard was gay?"

"Richard?" he asked, momentarily not sure who she was talking about. "Who's Richard?" Then the penny dropped. "Oh, you mean Kenty? Yeah, he's gay alright – bent as a nine-bob note. You don't want to waste any time on him. You're better off with a real man – like me."

If Kay hadn't known Glen better, she would scarcely have been able to believe what she was hearing. How on earth had she fallen for this idiot in her youth? She couldn't have been that naïve – could she? Yes, he had a fit body and good looks, but that was all he had in the plus column. His personality was nothing short of odious. As for his homophobic comments, this may have been over two decades ago but they were out of place even then. He seriously needed to be put in his place.

"Firstly," she began, "I know for a fact he isn't gay. Secondly, I find your homophobic comments nauseating. Perhaps you're the one who is gay, and you're trying to make out he is to cover up your own sexuality – have you considered that?"

She knew he wasn't, but it was fun winding him up saying it.

"Me? Gay? I've had more women than Kenty has had hot dinners," he boasted.

"Really?" she said. "Well, I'm sure they were very impressed by your ten-second performances. That is assuming, of course, that these fictional conquests exist – which I doubt. Quite honestly, it wouldn't surprise me one bit if you were still a virgin. And just in case you were wondering, if you haven't popped your cherry yet, you certainly won't be doing so with me."

Wow, it felt good saying this stuff. Twenty-five years of anger and resentment were pouring out of her onto her hapless victim in the doorway in front of her. She noticed that Glen was turning a deep shade of red. She could see that she was getting to him but wasn't finished yet.

"You seriously need to sort out your attitude to women – and people in general, come to that. You may think you're cool but anyone with half a brain cell can see what a twat you are a mile off. You can consider your invitation to the ball rescinded. I shall be making other arrangements."

Glen looked gobsmacked. He wasn't used to being spoken to like this. It was such a shock that he looked as if he was about to start crying.

"And don't even think about turning up and causing any trouble tonight or I'll tell all the girls at the ball that you've got a four-inch cock."

"How...how do you know?" he said, looking completely crestfallen.

"I have my ways and means," replied Kay. "Now, I suggest you go back upstairs and play with your little willy for a while because that's the only action you'll be getting today."

Satisfied that she had said enough, she turned on her heel and left, giving him a provocative wiggle of her arse as she did, just to show him what he would be missing. That was as near as he would be getting to her in this universe. What a pity this wasn't the real one.

Kay had said more than enough. The stuffing had been well and truly knocked out of him. It wasn't like Glen not to have the last word, but she had rendered him speechless. The only sound she heard behind her as she walked down the path was that of the door slamming, which set the neighbour's dog barking again.

She could consider part one of her plan well and truly complete. Now she could move on to make her next house call, one which she was expecting to be far more pleasant.

Chapter Ten
July 1994

Ten minutes later, Kay stood in front of Kent's house and pressed the bell. She had never been to his house before, but tracking him down hadn't been too difficult. Before she had left home that morning she had looked his address up in the telephone directory. Kent was not a very common name and there were only about a dozen in the book. She knew his father's name was David and there was only one with the initial 'D' in the book so it had to be him.

When he opened the door she could see that he wasn't fully dressed, just as Glen hadn't been. He didn't open the door fully, keeping his lower half behind the door and peering around it. That was fair enough, it was still pretty early in the day by teenage standards. She remembered that she rarely got up before lunchtime at that age if she didn't have to.

Kay could see enough of his top half to like what she saw. He was clad in a Blur T-shirt which showed not only his good taste in music but also his athletic frame.

Casting her eye appreciatively over him, she marvelled at how young and slim he was compared to the middle-aged boozer she had been speaking to in the pub the night before. She had forgotten just how good-looking he had been when he was young.

"Kay!" he exclaimed, just as surprised to see her as Glen had been. "What are you doing here?"

"Hi, Richard," she said. "Can I come in for a coffee and a quick chat?"

"Of course," he said, before adding, "The only thing is, I'm in my underpants. Can you hang on here a minute while I finish getting dressed?"

"That doesn't bother me," she said suggestively. "You don't have to leave me standing on the doorstep. I'm a big girl now." She enjoyed the irony of this statement, but it was of course lost on the young Kent.

He blushed, his shy and hormonal teenage self not yet experienced enough to deal with such blatant flirtation.

"Come on in, then," he said, letting go of the door. "I'll be back in a minute."

He scampered up the stairs in his kecks before she was barely over the threshold. Kay couldn't resist stealing a peek as he went and noted he was wearing briefs. That was interesting. Both Glen and Alan had preferred boxers. Could you tell what a man was like from his choice of underwear? Kay was always having these random thoughts.

She heard the unmistakable hiss of a deodorant upstairs and the running of a tap before he rushed back downstairs, only a couple of minutes after he had left. There was a blob of toothpaste on his T-shirt. Bless him – he was making an effort.

"How about this coffee, then?" she asked, unable to resist adding, "Preferably without any laxatives."

This comment was also meaningless to this version of Kent, who just looked at her with a perplexed expression on his face. She would have to stop dropping these little references into the conversation, as the last thing she wanted to do was make him uncomfortable.

"Joke," she explained. "Don't worry about it." She smiled at him to reassure him.

"Come through to the kitchen," he said. "You look lovely in that dress, by the way."

It was a genuine compliment, which she appreciated, and he had made it without ogling her breasts. As he busied himself preparing the coffee she made some small talk with him, asking him how his exams had gone and if he had any plans for university. Once they were both seated at the kitchen table, she decided it was time to get to the point.

"I expect you're wondering why I'm here," she said.

"It had crossed my mind," he replied. "Would you like a biscuit?" He offered her a round tartan tin and she took out a milk chocolate digestive. He seemed a little more relaxed than when she had first arrived.

"Well, it's quite simple really," she said, munching on her biscuit. "It's about the ball tonight."

"You're going with Glen, aren't you?" he said, not managing to conceal his disappointment.

"As it happens, no," replied Kay, and promptly launched into the tale of Glen's subterfuge.

"What a snake!" exclaimed Kent. "It doesn't surprise me, though. He's always screwing people over but I never thought he would do it to me. Fancy going around telling people that I'm gay! I'm supposed to be his best mate."

He looked pretty annoyed. Never mind, she had something much better to offer than his so-called best mate's fake friendship.

"Well, now you know what he is like, I suggest you don't get mad, but get even. That's where I come in."

He looked up hopefully, wondering what was coming next.

"What did you have in mind?" he asked.

"About the ball – did you manage to sort yourself out with a date?" asked Kay.

"Sadly not," he replied despondently. "Quite honestly, you were by far and away my first choice, and when that didn't work out, I didn't have the heart to ask anyone else."

"Well, it's all worked out nicely now," she said. "I've ditched him. So, Cinderella, it's your lucky night. That's if you still want to take me, of course."

His face lit up at her offer. "I'd love to," he said. "But should I do the dirty on a mate like that? It's not right, is it?"

"You mean your mate who treats women like shit and stabbed you in the back the first opportunity he got?" asked Kay.

"Well, when you put it like that," said Kent, "I'll be delighted to take you to the ball."

"Consider it a date," she replied. "And now that's all sorted, what are you up to today?"

She had only one day with him, so wanted to make all of it count.

"Well, nothing planned, really," he replied.

"You do now," she said. "I don't just want a date for the ball. I want you to be my boyfriend."

Kent was lost for words, scarcely able to believe his luck. Without further ado, she got up from her chair, walked over towards him, leant down and kissed him, sparing him the need to respond with words.

They kissed for about fifteen seconds. It was a pure, wonderful kiss, the sort that harkened back to times when a kiss wasn't merely the prelude to sex but enjoyable merely in itself. She had forgotten how amazing that felt.

Despite the purity of the moment, it could easily have led to more if she had wanted it to. She was sure he wouldn't resist if she took his hand right there and then and led him up the stairs, but she wanted more from the day than just sex. She wanted to spend the whole day getting to know this younger him, savouring the anticipation, before she seduced him at the end of the evening.

She broke off the kiss and jumped up. "Come on," she said. "If you're going to be my boyfriend, you can take me out for the day. Let's make it one to remember."

A day to remember it certainly was. They took the bus into Oxford, bought sandwiches from the M&S Foodhall, and had a picnic in Christ Church Meadow. They walked through the parks, holding hands, chatting and kissing in the sunshine. Then they hired a punt, something Kay had always wanted to do, and spent a lazy couple of hours on the River Cherwell. That was another box ticked off under things she had always meant to do but never got around to.

Later they went into town and browsed around some long-gone and fondly remembered shops. Cornmarket Street had never been the same for her since the day HMV had closed. Browsing through the racks of records and CDs they discovered that they had more than a few artists in common.

When the store started playing a recent Saint Etienne single and he remarked how much he liked them, she felt a rush of happiness at finding such a kindred spirit. He was everything she had hoped he would be and more. She would even go so far as to say she had found her soulmate. It was potentially heartbreaking that she had found him in the wrong universe and in the wrong time zone, but she tried not to think about that.

Before they got the bus home, they went to Old Orleans, Kay's all-time favourite restaurant in Oxford. It had stood on the corner of George Street just down from The Apollo for decades when Kay was growing up. She had been gutted when it had closed down in the late noughties.

As with HMV, she relished the opportunity to visit this old haunt one final time. Drawing fifty quid out of the cashpoint, she treated him to a meal. He was flattered and wanted to pay half, but she insisted. The money was of no future use to her in this world, so she may as well make use of it. And fifty quid went a long way in 1994.

She ordered a rib and wing combo, while Kent chose a steak. As they ate, they chatted away about every subject under the sun. The more they talked, the more she felt her affinity with him grow.

Smitten as she was, there was an unpleasant flip side to all of this that she was trying not to think about. Was she merely making things worse for herself by acting out this fantasy of what might have been? Was living this romantic dream right now going to make the pain of going home that much more unbearable when the time came?

Her feelings for him were becoming magnified with every passing moment. She couldn't remember feeling this intensely about anyone for a long time, but then, her feelings could be being enhanced by teenage hormones, something over which she had no control, even if her thoughts were those of a forty-three-year-old.

She had just about accepted that Kent couldn't be hers in the future before she had come here, but she knew that she was going to have to deal with those feelings all over again when she got back to 2018. No matter, she would just have to live with it. She remembered that old phrase: it was better to have loved and lost than never to have loved at all. Well, she was just going to have to give him his whole lifetime of loving in this one day.

Catching the bus home, they reluctantly parted for a couple of hours at teatime, returning home to get into their costumes. This allowed her to spend a little time with her parents. Her mother had made one of the gorgeous beef casseroles that had been Kay's favourite meal when she was growing up.

It was a serious case of pigging out on top of the meal she had eaten only an hour or so before in the restaurant, but there was no way she was missing the opportunity to enjoy her mother's cooking. It wasn't as if she had to worry about the extra calories either. Just like with spending all her money, she wouldn't have to worry about it later.

A moment on the lips, a lifetime on the hips, her mother used to say. Not today it wouldn't be. Kay hadn't eaten so well for months, living primarily off junk food since she had split with Alan. As long as she could still fit into her Catwoman costume after eating two dinners, she would be fine.

She enjoyed a great chat with her mum and dad over the meal, reminiscing about some of the holidays they had had when she was a kid. She wished she could have spent more time with them, but tonight was all about her and Kent. There would be more opportunities for family time later. She already had an idea in mind.

As soon as she had eaten, she headed upstairs to make herself look beautiful – not that she needed to. Looking at herself in the mirror, she had to admit that she looked amazing. She was a flower in full bloom before the inevitably of ageing had made that flower begin to wither. There was no going back for most people, just a long, slow decline into death. But Kay briefly had been given the chance to bloom afresh, and here she was now, dressed to kill in her Catwoman outfit.

Almost ready to go, she checked her handbag, making sure she had stowed the pack of condoms inside. She had been keeping them in her bedside table as a teenager for just such an occasion. Just as with the money she had spent and the calories she had consumed, she was aware that when it came to sex, taking precautions had no consequences in this temporary universe. But she would take them, anyway. This version of Kent didn't know that his world wasn't real and if he wanted to use protection, she had to respect that.

Most men didn't want to use condoms in her experience, despite all the warnings. Perhaps it was down to some sort of primaeval urge to ensure their sperm hit the target. Then again, perhaps the men she had been with were not representative of the population as a whole, considering that she generally picked arseholes. Nearly all of them either conveniently forgot or made up some bullshit like Glen had about being allergic to latex.

Kent was right on time calling for her, and within an hour they were at the ball. Of Glen, there was no sign. It seemed he had wisely heeded her advice and stayed away to avoid any further humiliation. Despite all his bravado, he was clearly a complete coward when someone stood up to him like Kay had.

Kay couldn't have hoped for a better evening. It wouldn't have been an exaggeration to say that it was the happiest day of her life, and that included her wedding day, which hadn't been all that great. How could it have been? She had been lumbering herself with Alan for twenty years.

This night may have been taking place in a fake universe, but in Kay's eyes, it would always be real. The memories she was making tonight would be precious, and she would be able to carry them with her for the rest of her life. Nothing could take them away from her.

She and Kent were inseparable all evening, cherishing every single moment together. Of course, he had no way of knowing that it was only for one night. It seemed almost cruel in a way. Was it right of the angel to create new universes at will and then delete them at her leisure?

Was that not tantamount to murdering the people who lived in those new universes, even if their counterparts lived on in the original? Who was to say? At least in Kent's case, ignorance was bliss. He was deliriously happy at what was happening, unaware that he would soon cease to exist.

At least there was another Kent, the original one back in 2018 who had got to live his own version of this day again. She wondered how he had felt when he returned. Had he fallen for her in that timeline, just as he had in this one? It would certainly explain why he had been so much kinder to her in recent weeks in the real world.

In this world, the evening was racing past far too quickly for Kay's liking. It seemed like no time at all until they were sharing the last dance of the night, a smoochy ballad from Wet Wet Wet. As the song came to a close, she knew it was time to tell him what she wanted to say and what she hoped he wanted to hear. She whispered into his ear, "I want to come home with you tonight."

He didn't resist, just as she had hoped. Within an hour of that final dance, the two of them were making love in his bed. The contrast with the original version of this night could not have been greater. Glen had wanted her purely for sex: this was different. This was more like the movie sex she had always believed was a myth. No man had ever gazed into her eyes before in the way that he did. It was without a doubt the most intimate experience of her life.

Later they held each other tightly, cuddled up in the afterglow. This wasn't something she was used to, either. Alan used to just roll over and go to sleep straight after sex and none of her one-night stands during the past year had shown her the slightest bit of affection.

Right at that moment, curled up with Kent, she had never felt so close to another human being in all her life. She tried desperately to cling to the moment and stay awake as long as she could, willing the angel not to take her back, but in her warm and contented state, sleep soon came.

Chapter Eleven
December 2018

The next thing she knew, she was back in the bathroom in her flat. It was all over. Strangely, she didn't feel sad at being dragged back to reality. Instead, she felt a sense of triumph. She had achieved everything she had set out to do and the results had massively exceeded her expectations.

She turned to the mirror, a smile on her face.

The angel was waiting for her.

"That's the happiest I've seen you," remarked her reflection.

"It should be," said Kay. "I've just had the most amazing day of my entire life. Whatever happens in the future, nothing and nobody can take that away from me now."

"That's great to hear," remarked the angel. "I can see that my presence here is doing some good."

"I'm very grateful," said Kay. And she meant it. What the angel was doing for her was starting to turn her life around.

After two trips back in time her head was brimming with ideas. Her easy disposal of Glen had made her keen to serve up some just deserts to Alan, too, but she wanted more than the satisfaction of some short-term revenge. Kent's tale of his antics with the dinosaur had made her think of all sorts of humiliating pranks she could pull on Alan, but it would only be a brief moment of satisfaction, and that wasn't enough. She wanted to do something in the past that could make a tangible difference to her life here in the present.

"That's what I'm here for," said the angel. "It's good to see you making good use of your days."

"There's plenty more I want to do yet," she said.

"So I see," replied the angel, probing her thoughts. "You're a smart girl. I can see you are looking at ways to make the most of this experience. Not everybody does. Far too many just squander it on pleasure-seeking and trivial things."

"Well, I've got a good idea what I want to do next," said Kay. "But I'm not sure I might not be breaking the rules doing it."

"It's not physically possible to break any rules," replied the angel. "There's no way to cheat the system – say, to smuggle some money forward through time, for example."

"I realise that," said Kay, "Though what I have in mind does involve money."

"I can see what you're thinking and there's nothing to say you can't do it," said the angel. "Just keep in mind the physical limitations of what you are trying to achieve. The golden rules remain set in stone. You can't take anything into the past with you and you can't bring anything back from the past into the present day. If you can figure out a way that works around that, then I would say go for it."

"I will," replied Kay. She would certainly figure it out. The angel was right. She was still that smart, clever nineteen-year-old inside, despite the wasted years since. It was time to put that intelligence to good use.

"Well, you have all day to think about your plans," said the angel. "Good luck." The image of Kay's younger self faded from the mirror, to be replaced by her present-day reflection once again.

She could spend the day at work thinking about what she was going to do and then run it by Kent in the evening. Despite it being Sunday, it was no day of rest for her. This was the ninth day of ten in a row that she was working, up to and including Christmas Eve. She needed every penny she could get, especially with the pressure McVie had been putting on her.

She hated the job, but no matter. It was only two more days. Then, hopefully, she would be finished with it forever. She was formulating a big plan to get her out of this mess, and this next trip could be the key that would unlock her future.

She had an earlier finish at work with it being a Sunday, the store closing at 4pm. Despite that, it was already dark when she left the shop not long after, and remarkably there was snow beginning to fall. Surely they couldn't be in for a white Christmas, could they? She had waited her whole life to see one. They happened in every Christmas movie or festive TV special she had ever seen, but never in real life.

Snow or not, maybe this Christmas was going to be the one when all her dreams would come true. As she walked up the street, watching the light, powdery snowflakes lit up by the glow from the street's Christmas lights, she began to feel quite festive. Yes, this was going to be a Christmas to remember. Or possibly even two. She had come up with an idea that would enable her to uniquely enjoy two Christmas Days this year.

Arriving at the shop, she could see that it hadn't yet opened for the evening. McVie usually shut it for a few hours in the afternoon, opening again at about 5pm for the teatime rush.

When Kay was young, it would have been unheard of for a chip shop to open on a Sunday. Her family, like most others, always sat down to a traditional roast dinner on that day. It seemed that people didn't bother so much with that anymore. Most shops and fast-food places were now open seven days a week. Kay thought that was a shame – she had liked it when Sunday had been special. Now it was just a day like any other.

The lights were on inside the shop, but the door was still locked. She let herself in with her key, not happy to see her dreaded landlord behind the counter after the way he had harassed her the day before. He had his back to her and was once again berating Anna, the young Polish girl.

She could see that Anna was clearing away some of the uneaten food from the lunchtime session, but McVie was having none of it.

"What the fuck do you think you're doing?" he said, as Anna removed a crusty, dried-up fish cake from the glass cabinets with a pair of tongs, and turned to put it in the bin.

"These have been here all afternoon," replied Anna in her perfect English. "The cabinets have been switched off for two hours."

"I know," replied McVie. "I switched them off. Do you know how much electricity those things burn? Now put that back in there right now. That's pure profit you're throwing in the bin there – profit that keeps me in business and you in a job.

Reluctantly, Anna complied, but added, "What about health and safety?"

"Bollocks to health and safety," replied McVie. "Cook some fresh ones and hide that one back in among them. Then make sure you give that one to some old pensioner. If it is dodgy and they end up croaking, no one will get suspicious. It'll just get blamed on the cold weather. They drop like flies at this time of year."

Kay stood watching this exchange, unnoticed by McVie who was still facing away from her. She caught Anna's eye, who gave her a resigned look as she reluctantly complied. Meanwhile, McVie poked around in the bin.

"What else have you chucked in here?" he asked. Then he pulled out a jumbo sausage.

"What are you doing throwing this away? There's nothing wrong with this. Two quid, these sell for. You can put that back, too."

"It's dirty," said Anna.

McVie pulled a piece of blue tissue paper from a roll behind the counter, and turned, wiping down the sausage. "There. It's as good as new."

As he spoke, he caught sight of Kay for the first time.

"Here you are, why don't you sell it to this bitch? She likes getting her lips around a big sausage, from what I've heard. Tell you what, since I know you're hard up, missy, you can have it for half-price."

Kay was in no mood to be trifled with.

"Do the food and hygiene people know you sell food out of the bin?" she asked.

"Why, are you going to tell them?" said McVie, leaning over the counter towards her, aggressively. "Take a look at the front door, darling. Five-star hygiene rating, that's what I've got here. Who are they going to believe – me, a respectable local business owner, or you, some drunken slag with barely two pennies to rub together?"

Kay could easily have lost her rag with him right there and then, but she forced herself to play it cool. She needed to hold onto her flat for a couple more days, just long enough for her to take another trip or two. If all went according to plan, he could stick his flat after that.

"Forget it," she said, resisting the temptation to tell him to shove the jumbo sausage up his arse, Kent-style. "I'm going upstairs."

"Don't forget I want that rent by tomorrow night," he said. "Or the electricity goes off and you'll be eating raw Bernard Matthews turkey roll for your Christmas dinner."

"Whatever," said Kay, opening the door at the back of the shop and swiftly closing it again behind her. What a disgusting excuse for a human being McVie was. She may have to think of a way of sorting him out, too, once she had dealt with Alan.

She was tired out by her recent adventures and the long day at work, so she decided to get her head down for an hour and have a power nap. It was an apt description. Never in her life had she had any real power, but now she had plenty. The gift the angel had given her was potentially more powerful than any position or amount of money if she used it wisely.

If she did manage to pull off her audacious plan, she may soon be enjoying a siesta as opposed to a power nap. Technically that's what this was, having a sleep in the afternoon, but she could hardly call an hour in a freezing flat in pitch darkness a siesta. It was a far cry from snoozing in the Spanish sun on a baking afternoon.

As she drifted off to sleep, she vowed to herself soon she would be there, enjoying her time in the sun. As soon as all this was over, she intended to get herself off to the Canaries for some much-needed winter warmth. Such a trip was completely out of the question in her current perilous financial position, but that situation was something she intended to change.

She awoke after an hour or so and began to prepare herself to go out. Kent had promised to meet her in the pub to talk about the trip she had just taken and she was feeling very excited about it.

She wasn't going to hold back any information about her day and she hoped he would do the same. It would be fascinating to see what similarities and differences there had been between there two experiences.

Feeling refreshed and happy, she prepared to leave the flat, full of anticipation for the night ahead.

Chapter Twelve
December 2018

At 8.30pm she walked into the bar of The Red Lion to be greeted by an unholy cacophony of noise coming from the back of the pub. Some fat, dark-haired woman she didn't recognise in her thirties was belting out a truly awful rendition of an old Abba song.

The pub was very busy for a Sunday, but then it was only two days until Christmas. There was quite a crowd gathered around the DJ booth at the far end of the dance floor where, despite the bad singing, it seemed the karaoke was going down a storm. As the woman finished her song, she was met with a huge round of applause. The audience must be tone-deaf, drunk, or both.

"Wow, what a performance!" announced the DJ, a rotund man in his late forties with thickset glasses. "I don't know how we're going to top that, but we'll give it a go! Next up, please can we have The Three Drunken Twats?"

Amid much laughing, three young lads headed up to the stage. There was plenty of festive spirit around tonight, it seemed.

Kay made her way over to the bar. Andy was there, talking to his mate, Nobby, who as always was immaculately dressed and groomed. He was the only person Kay had ever seen wearing a suit in the pub. There was no sign of Kent.

When Kay got to the bar, Craig greeted her much more enthusiastically than usual. It made a welcome change. He had been a right miserable sod recently.

"What do you think of the karaoke, then?" he asked. "I told you it would be a winner. I'm thinking of having it every Sunday."

"I bloody hope not," interrupted Nobby. "Because if you do I'll be drinking elsewhere. That last woman was dreadful. Her voice was like squeaky chalk on a blackboard. And now listen to this lot!"

The lads who had formed the impromptu group called The Three Drunken Twats had embarked on a rendition of "The Twelve Days of Christmas". It sounded more like it was being sung from the terraces at Old Trafford than over a microphone. Everyone watching was in hysterics, especially when one of them made an obscene gesture in response to the line "Five gold rings".

"Well, I think it's quite funny," said Kay, who wasn't averse to the odd spot of karaoke. "I may even have a go myself after a few drinks. Speaking of which…"

As she had been speaking, she had pulled a tenner out of her purse and handed it to Craig who had already poured her a double vodka as soon as he had seen her heading towards the bar.

"You did want the usual, I take it?" he asked.

"Of course," she said. She would have to resist the temptation to knock it straight back. She would have to make it last. This tenner was all the money she had left in the world for the time being.

"Can you fill it up to the top with Coke," she asked. That would make it last a bit longer.

"No problem," replied Craig.

"Have you seen Richard tonight?" she asked him, trying to say it quietly so that Andy wouldn't hear.

"Who's Richard?" replied Craig, turning back towards her, vodka and Coke in hand. It was the second time today she had received that response. Was she the only person in the world who knew his first name? Why did people only ever refer to him by his surname? She thought it was rather rude. He deserved better.

"Sorry, I mean Kent," said Kay.

"He hasn't been in yet," said Craig. "Listen, why don't you put your name down for the karaoke? Even this idiot here is having a go." He gesticulated towards Andy.

"Less of the idiot, if you don't mind," replied Andy.

"You are an idiot," said Craig, but then added, almost affectionately, "but you're our idiot."

He was in an uncharacteristic good mood. She couldn't remember him ever saying anything nice about Andy before.

But that was down to the generally happy atmosphere in the pub tonight. Andy seemed happy with Craig's response and turned around to continue his conversation with Nobby.

"Yeah, I'll give it a go," said Kay to Craig.

"Go over and see Jason, the DJ, and put your name down ASAP, then," said Craig. "There's quite a waiting list by the looks of things."

Kay took her drink and wandered over to the stage area by the DJ booth where The Three Drunken Twats had just finished their song to great acclaim from the crowd. She waited patiently while the DJ blathered on in a lame attempt at a stand-up comedy routine before calling up the next singer.

It was a young girl next whom she recognised as Lauren, a short, dark-haired girl with a cheeky grin and jet-black hair styled in a bob. She was wearing an extremely low-cut, black top that left very little to the imagination.

Kay observed the crowd's reaction with amusement as the lively young girl began to sing. The assembled group of lads watching had eyes on stalks as Lauren launched into the old Katy Perry number, "I Kissed a Girl". She played up very suggestively to the crowd, boobs practically spilling out of her top, and even pulled over a girlfriend at one point and kissed her squarely on the lips, sending the boys into a frenzy.

She knows how to get male attention, thought Kay, wistfully remembering how it had once been like that for her.

She hoped Lauren would have more luck with men in the long run than she had.

Kay managed to get the DJ's attention and gave him her song choice, then turned back to the bar where she was thrilled to see that Kent had now arrived and was standing with the others.

She rushed straight back over to the bar to see him, a move that wasn't unnoticed by Andy.

"Here comes your girlfriend," remarked Andy to Kent. "I wouldn't like to be in your shoes when your missus finds out."

"Shut up, Andy," said Kent. "You don't know what you're talking about." Taking his freshly poured pint of bitter, he said to Kay, "Come on, let's go somewhere we can talk."

"Another cosy chat in the corner, is it?" called Andy after them. "This is getting to be a bit of a habit."

They ignored him and moved to the table at the front of the pub where they had sat the previous evening, far enough away from the karaoke to be able to hear each other speak without shouting.

"I don't want to be too long," said Kent. "Debs wasn't too happy about me coming out tonight, but I had to find out how it went. Tell me all about it."

Kay described in detail the events of the previous day. Kent listened, smiling, chuckling and commenting at certain points.

"I would have loved to have been a fly on the wall when you told Glen where to get off," he said. "Has he really only got a four-inch cock? That's hilarious!"

"I'm afraid so," she replied. "No wonder he used to show off so much: it was probably his way of compensating for his inadequacies down there."

"That's made my day, that has," said Kent.

"I thought it would," said Kay, resisting the temptation to say, "Yours was much bigger." That might have been interpreted as flirting which she was trying to cut out.

Later he exclaimed, "I loved Old Orleans!" as Kay described their day out in Oxford. "I so miss that place. They used to do amazing cocktails."

At the end of her story, she didn't hold anything back. As she described what had happened when they had gone back to his room, she held his gaze, looking into his eyes just as she had with her younger self in his bed.

But this was an older Kent and a different Kent. He broke her gaze, looking nervously down into his drink.

"What's the matter?" she said. "Didn't the same happen when you went back to relive that day?"

"Yes," he admitted, almost furtively. "But it's different for you. You're single now. I'm married. It's still sort of cheating, in a way."

"But that didn't bother you when you went back before, did it?" she questioned.

"No, but it was different then. I was going back in my own timeline, to my youth. I never thought in a million years I'd be sitting here having this conversation with you in the present day. Now that you've had the same experience, it somehow makes it more real."

She could see that she needed to reassure him. "Look, it's OK," she said. "You know I fancy you like crazy, always have done, but I respect the fact that you're married. I'm not a threat to you."

"You say that now," replied Kent. "But what about later when you've had a few drinks? How many times have you drunkenly tried to lure me back to your flat?"

Kay couldn't blame him for thinking that based on her past behaviour. What sort of woman had she turned into? She would not have dreamt of messing around with a married man in her youth. She must have acquired a terrible reputation around town.

She knew she had because the woman who had knocked her teeth out had seen to that. She had named and shamed Kay all over Facebook on the town chat page. Admin had swiftly deleted it, but the damage had been done.

She must stick to the vow she had made a couple of days ago. There must be no more married men, and that included Kent. Despite the way the flame inside her for him was burning as strongly as ever, she knew deep down it could never be. She finally felt that she was able to accept that now. Perhaps the trip to the past had got it out of her system.

They were friends now and that was the next-best thing in a world which had by and large turned against her. She could not risk losing that friendship, especially now, when she could benefit greatly from his help and advice. He had more experience than her of travelling back through time, and she wanted to bounce some more ideas off him.

"You don't need to worry about that anymore," she said. "I've got it out of my system now, honestly. I just want to be friends." It hurt having to say these words, but it was the only way if she was to get him to trust her.

He seemed to relax after that and open up a bit, offering some observations on their unusual situation.

"You know, we've had a relationship that is probably unique in the whole history of the world," he said.

"How do you mean?" she asked.

"It's really strange when you think about it," he said. "We've both slept with each other, but we both haven't if you get what I mean. I've slept with another version of you. You've slept with another version of me. But us two here talking right now haven't slept with each other."

"Weird, isn't it?" replied Kay. "But I like it. All these billions of people in the world, and as far as we know, no one else has ever had the same experience."

"So, now that's out of the way, what's next?" asked Kent, clearly keen to hear what she had planned for tomorrow.

"Well, that's the other thing I wanted to talk to you about," said Kay.

She filled him in on the backstory of her break-up with Alan and how he was dragging his heels over the divorce proceedings. She also explained how she believed he had been hiding funds from her and how she planned to use one of her trips to investigate.

"That's an inspired idea," said Kent. "After I realised I couldn't change history, I never really explored the possibility of solving mysteries in my past. I had enough difficulty doing detective work in the present, to be honest. That's probably why I am now unemployed."

"So what's the legality of me poking around in his past affairs?" she asked.

"I'm not sure of the exact legal position of it all, that's more for lawyers than policemen. I do know that opening other people's emails etc. can be considered an invasion of privacy, but that normally revolves around corporate spying or identity theft. As far as domestic cases go, in all my years in the force, no one ever came into the station and accused their husband or wife of such a thing. Besides, you'll be in the other universe, so it doesn't matter even if you do get caught snooping around somewhere you shouldn't."

"Sounds like there's nothing to worry about, then," said Kay. "I can concentrate on the most important thing, which is to find the evidence in the first place."

"That's another thing I meant to bring up – the question of evidence," replied Kent.

"Go on," said Kay.

"Well, even if you did find any evidence in the past, as I am sure you must know by now, you can't bring it back to the present to use against him. It's difficult to see what you can effectively do."

"What if I buried it or hid it somewhere, ready for me to dig up when I return?" she asked.

"That wouldn't work either," he said. "You go back into Universe 2.0, remember? It wouldn't be there for you to dig up in Universe 1.0."

"Of course, it wouldn't," she said, mentally kicking herself for making such an obvious mistake. "You must think I'm a right numpty for that suggestion."

"Of course not," said Kent. "You're still learning and there's a lot to get your head around. Time travel is a complicated business. It wasn't until at least my third trip that I got to grips with it all. I didn't even realise you couldn't change history until after the second. The angel didn't bother to tell me that and I wasted a whole trip on a fruitless gambling spree thinking I could make myself rich."

"So it looks like I'm going to be relying on my memory," said Kay. "That's if I can even find anything."

"Your memory is all you've got. It's the one thing you can take with you through time. What you need to do is to go back to a time when he won't suspect that you know anything," said Kent. "Pick a date before you broke up: that way you'll be still living in your house and will have free rein to investigate."

"That makes sense," replied Kay. "I can't go round there now, he's changed the locks. He did it the day after I moved out. That makes me even more suspicious that he's got something to hide. He clearly didn't want me going back there and poking around in his secret office. He pretty much locked me out of there even before we split up."

"You also don't want him around while you are doing your snooping," added Kent. "Make sure you pick a day when he won't be there."

"That shouldn't be too difficult," replied Kay. "He was always off on his business trips. That's if they even were business trips. Half the time I suspect he was holed up in some hotel somewhere with that tart, Lucy. I'm convinced he was having an affair with her for months, if not years, before he kicked me out. That's something else I can probably find proof of, now I think about it."

"It sounds like you have got the makings of a decent plan there, then," said Kent. "Part of me wishes I was coming with you. I miss travelling to the past now it's over."

"Well, I will tell you all about it when I get back," said Kay, happy with the way the conversation had gone. "Shall we go back to the bar now?"

"Well, I really ought to be getting home," replied Kent. "I told Debs I was only going out for one. But then, when have I ever done that? It hardly seems worth coming out just for one, does it? And it is Christmas, after all."

"Agreed," said Kay. "I can only afford one more, though, that's if I'm going to eat tomorrow."

"I'll get you one," he said. "That's what friends are for."

Gratefully she accepted and they went to the bar. His comment about them being friends had given her a warm feeling inside because she knew he meant it. Real friends had been sorely lacking from her life for a long time, but now she knew for sure that she had at least one. Perhaps one was all you needed if they stood by you. She truly felt that in his case, he would.

It was worth their while staying, purely for the entertainment value of seeing Andy's botched attempt at resurrecting his rockstar past. He was doing surprisingly well with his rendition of "Born to be Wild" – at least he was until he got to the second chorus when he tripped over the microphone stand and fell flat on his face, bringing an inevitable cheer from the crowd.

"Look out for that one on YouTube tomorrow!" announced the DJ. "It's not the first time he's done that and it won't be the last. Andy Green – we salute you – what a star!"

Kay downed the remainder of her drink and got ready to leave. She went home feeling full of the joys of the season, looking forward to the challenge that lay ahead the next day.

Chapter Thirteen
February 2018

By the time the angel appeared in the mirror the following morning, Kay was all prepared with the exact date she needed to go back to.

Compared to her previous trips, this would be just a short hop in temporal terms. Her destination was February 14th 2018, a day she remembered well.

It had been a Wednesday and she had been looking forward to going out for a meal with Alan, something they had done every Valentine's Day since they had got together.

Date nights such as these had become increasingly rare in recent years. Other than Valentine's Day, the only other time they went out for a meal was for their wedding anniversary. It was all a far cry from the wining and dining he had done to impress her in the early days.

This year, the meal had not happened at all. A couple of days beforehand, he had announced that some major problem had come up with a wine supplier at work and he was going to have to fly to Paris the following day to sort it out.

When she had suggested going with him, Alan had not looked happy. He had said that he would love to have her accompany him, but the company was having financial difficulties and he wouldn't be able to justify a ticket for her on expenses. Besides, he would be spending all day in crisis meetings trying to resolve the problems, followed by dinner with the suppliers in the evenings. He wouldn't be able to spend any time with her, so there was no point in her going.

This had unsurprisingly turned out to be complete bullshit. By this time, Kay had already suspected him of having an affair, so disappearing off on Valentine's Day set all sorts of alarm bells ringing in her head.

A few weeks later he had told her he didn't think the marriage was working out and had ordered her to move out. She was barely out of the door before he installed the hated Lucy in her place. It didn't take a genius to work out it was her that he had spent that week in Paris with.

As for Kay, she stayed at home and spent Valentine's Day watching old Bridget Jones movies on DVD. She didn't hear a peep from Alan all day, and as for any sort of Valentine's present, that was a joke. She didn't even get a card.

His absence that day was just what she needed to carry out her detective work. He would be nicely out of the way in Paris with that red-headed tart, enabling her to snoop at her leisure.

Maddie would also be out of the way, spending half-term visiting some friends in London. At eighteen, she had inherited Kay's adventurous streak, also expressing a desire to go travelling after her A levels. Kay just hoped she wouldn't fall prey to another Glen, or even worse, another Alan.

With the house to herself, she could take her time and leave no stone unturned. It wasn't going to be one of the most exciting days of her life, but this time she was putting business before pleasure. This was about looking to the future, not reliving the past. If she found what she was looking for, then her unsuspecting victim would have his revenge served up cold just in time for Christmas.

Kay didn't bother with any preamble with the angel, telling her where she wanted to go right away. She soon found herself waking up in the past for the third time, in a third different bed. She was exactly where she had expected to be – in the house that had been her home until just a few months ago.

How she missed this room. She hadn't seen the inside of it since the day she had left. Her former home was a four-bedroom townhouse on one of the town's new estates. Compared to the flat above McVie's, it was a mansion. They had bought it three years before as a new build. After reserving the plot, they had the opportunity to have a say in all of the final specifications. That had allowed her to properly put her stamp on it.

Her bedroom, which on the plans had been described as the master bedroom, was an impressive size by modern standards, a spacious room where there was plenty of floor space, even with the king-size bed against the back wall.

Every bit of furnishing in the room had been chosen and bought by her. Alan was not interested in those sorts of cosmetic details and had left her to get on with it. She had decorated and furnished it to what she felt was perfection. All of the furniture was made of pine, from the bed frame to the bedside tables. It was good, solid stuff, not like the cheap, flimsy rubbish they sold in some stores.

The walls of the room were a pale lemon colour, with curtains to match. It was a similar shade to the dress she had recently worn in 1994. Yellow had always been her favourite colour.

The massive windows along the left-hand side of the room made it wonderfully light, even on this winter morning. The whole of the opposite side of the room was taken up by a large, walk-in wardrobe, full of clothes. Most of these she hadn't been able to take with her when she left. Alan had allowed her to pack just one suitcase before he escorted her off the premises the day she had left. When she tried to get back in a few days later, she discovered that he had changed the locks.

It made her sick to the stomach to think that it was now Lucy who got to wake up in this room every day. It was Lucy who got to bounce up and down on top of her mattress on top of her husband. It was Lucy who had taken over her room, her territory and her man, like some foreign power mercilessly marching its army across her borders to annex her territory.

Well, Lucy was in for a surprise, just as much as Alan was. Legally, Kay still owned half of this house, despite Alan's best attempts to screw it out of her in the divorce. Yes, he may have earned far more than she had during the years they had been together, but there was more than a marriage to that.

Kay had kept house for him, raised their daughter practically single-handedly, and done pretty much everything else for him since the day they had moved in together. In her eyes, that had just as much value as actual money being put on the table. His ducking and diving to get out of giving her any money in the divorce was unforgivable. She was simply not going to let him get away with it.

She dressed, freshened up, and went downstairs for breakfast. She noticed in the bathroom that the laundry basket was full and almost instinctively went to put a wash load on before remembering that she didn't have to. She didn't have to concern herself with any of that today. By 10am, she was ready to get started with what she had come here to do.

Her focus would be entirely on one room on the middle floor of the house. With only three of them living there, four bedrooms had been a luxury. Alan had quickly suggested that one of them become his office for when he worked from home. This had seemed a perfectly reasonable suggestion at the time. They certainly didn't need two guest bedrooms. The only time they ever had anyone to stay was when one of Maddie's friends would come for a sleepover.

It hadn't taken him long to become extremely protective over his office. He installed a desk, computer, filing cabinet and even a safe. When she questioned what he needed a safe for, he spun her some yarn about company policy when handling confidential documents.

Not long afterwards he informed her that she didn't need to clean the room: he would do it himself. It was the first time in his life he had ever offered to help with the housework. If that hadn't been enough to make it crystal clear he didn't want her in there, a few weeks later he installed a lock on the door. She had never seen the key. He justified this as being in the interests of security. He said he couldn't rule out rival firms breaking into the house and trying to steal company secrets.

What utter rot, thought Kay now, as she stood in front of the locked door. Well, whatever secrets he was keeping in there, they were not going to remain secret much longer.

The only way she was going to get in was by giving the door a good kicking. She hoped that, as it was only an internal door, it wouldn't put up too much resistance. It always looked so easy when people did it on the telly. To make sure, she headed into Maddie's bedroom and borrowed a big, heavy pair of boots that she insisted were all the fashion, though Kay thought they looked hideous.

The boots proved to be very useful. They had steel toecaps and two good kicks at the lock got the door open. Although it was a pretty solid lock, he hadn't installed it particularly well and it splintered easily.

DIY was one of many things Alan wasn't much good at. He argued that he was a professional businessman who didn't need to learn manual skills, as people like him paid other people to do those sorts of jobs. In reality, due to his incredible stinginess when it came to parting with cash, it had been Kay who had ended up doing most of the maintenance around the house.

With the door open, Kay ventured forward eagerly into his man cave, wondering what she would find. At first glance, the room was nothing out of the ordinary. It was pretty much as it had looked when she had last seen it, which had been a good couple of years ago. He had been very meticulous in keeping her out of the office, even locking the door when he was working.

She noticed right away how dusty all the surfaces were, including the laptop keyboard which was also covered in crumbs and flakes of what looked like dead skin. There were also several dead flies on the windowsill. So much for cleaning the room himself, she thought.

Where should she start? She went for the laptop first. It was switched off so before she booted it up, she grabbed a couple of wipes and gave it a quick clean. There was no way she was touching that in its current state. Then she turned it on and waited, expecting to face some sort of password protection.

Sure enough, the welcome screen was soon replaced by another asking for a PIN. That was potentially easier than a password. She could have a reasonable stab at guessing it. What would he use?

He had been born on the 25th October 1964, so she tentatively typed in 2510. To her amazement, the screen changed to the standard Windows opening screen. She had guessed correctly at the first attempt!

She couldn't believe it. What an absolute muppet! Why go to all this effort to secure the room and then use his birthday as his PIN? Even Kay, who wasn't that tech-savvy, knew that you never used your date of birth as a PIN or a password. It was one of the first things that hackers would try.

Cracking his code was going to make her job a whole lot easier. The laptop must be full of clues, especially if he had been labouring under the false premise that it was secure. So, what should she look for first?

Her primary goal was to find out more about his financial affairs, in particular, if he was hiding any money from her. However, she couldn't resist checking out his Facebook first. He had left it logged in so she didn't have to worry about a password.

She went straight to his messages and found what she was looking for right away – a stash of private messages between him and Lucy. She steeled herself for what she might find as she opened it up. It was everything she was expecting: declarations of love, oodles of kisses, hearts and other emojis, mostly from her to him.

As she scrolled up there was also a lot of dirty talk, describing what they were planning to do to each other. She didn't bother reading all of it. There was too much for a start, an additional 1,384 messages above. The affair had been going on for a long time. She decided to just skim through the last few, most of which related to their Paris plans.

One phrase in his last message read:

Haha, don't worry, the stupid cow doesn't suspect a thing. See you in the morning x x

She had replied with a graphic of two champagne glasses clinking and lots of hearts.

Kay was pleased that she didn't feel in the remotest bit upset by reading any of this. That was good: it meant that she must be over him. She was also amused to see that Lucy's messages were full of spelling mistakes and bad grammar. She was obviously not the brightest tool in the box.

"Enjoy your champagne while you can," she murmured. "This stupid cow is about to come back and bite you on the arse big time."

What else could she find? She opened up his emails and scrolled through them. Nothing sprang out at her. It was mainly marketing stuff from various companies he had dealt with.

It was time to look around the rest of the office. She turned her attention to his filing cabinet next. It was one of those big, grey, metal ones with four drawers, just like you would find in the average office. She tried to open the top drawer, only to discover it was locked. So where might be the key? Would he keep it on him? She hoped not, otherwise she was going to have to try and break into it and it was made of pretty solid metal. Hopefully, the key would be somewhere in the room.

There was a drawer in his desk which she was pleased to discover was not locked. It was full of stationery and other

156

assorted crap such as loose batteries, random cables, and half-eaten packets of sweets. There was also a small, old-fashioned toffee tin which she had seen him with before. She remembered that he used to keep his golf tees in it. She picked it up and shook it, making it rattle.

She took the lid off, and nestling in amongst the golf tees was a small metal key. He hadn't been very imaginative in hiding that. She took the key and tried it in the cabinet. She felt a real sense of satisfaction as she felt it turn with ease. His security measures were no match for a wife who knew him inside out.

The cabinet was full of files, none of them labelled. She would just have to go through each in turn until she found what she was looking for. She didn't know exactly what that was, just that she would know when she found it.

Over the next hour or so, she pulled out each file in turn and went through the contents. A lot of it was very boring stuff to do with work: store design plans and sales data for various products. There was also a lot of documentation relating to the house. This mainly consisted of stacks of old utility bills and endless instruction manuals for various kettles, toasters and other domestic appliances that they had bought over the years.

There was even one for a VHS player they had bought in the 1990s, which they must have disposed of well over a decade ago when DVDs had rendered it obsolete.

Just as she was beginning to despair she might not find anything useful, she found a folder full of recent credit card and bank statements. This was a lot more promising.

The credit card statements proved to be extremely interesting reading. They were full of sizeable payments to hotel companies stretching back over the past couple of years.

She also found several of the accompanying hotel bills. One glance at them with their itemised details of room service and champagne was more than enough evidence that his affair with Lucy the illiterate had been going on for a good, long while. They stretched back at least two years.

Kay couldn't care less about the affair now, but she could see that there had been no expense spared on these hotel trips. That was something that did annoy her. It was out of character with his skinflint nature that she had grown to despise over the years.

Only the previous summer, she remembered how tight he had been over money on their holiday. It was the first time they had been away together for a proper break without Maddie since she had been born, but it hadn't been a lot of fun.

During their week in Marbella, he had been moody and miserable throughout, doubtless because he was missing his whore of a girlfriend. No wonder he had spent so much of that week pissing about on his phone – he was probably messaging her the whole time.

He had pleaded poverty throughout that week in Marbella, constantly moaning about the crap exchange rate since Brexit. On the first night, he had informed her that he was setting them a budget for their main evening meal of thirty euros per night.

He was incredibly mean about how he enforced it, too. One night they had dined at a nice little restaurant by the harbour. Perusing the menu, he had decided he wanted to treat himself to a fillet steak, the most expensive item on the menu at twenty-two euros. He then informed her that to stay within their budget, she was not allowed to spend more than eight euros on her main. So she ended up having an omelette.

That was just one example of his tightness. He was forever badgering her about saving money on the shopping and wouldn't let her shop in any supermarket other than the chain he worked at, even though she much preferred Sainsbury's. He said it was financial madness to go shopping anywhere else when they could take advantage of his staff discount.

His controlling nature often extended to coming along on the weekly shop, making her pick cheap brands and reduced items on things she wanted to buy. He even made her buy the supermarket's own-brand tampons, rather than the brand she preferred, claiming they were just as good. As if he would know.

When they got to the booze aisle he would then proceed to pick himself out a couple of £10 bottles of red wine, which he would claim was a treat. This was of no benefit to Kay as she only drank white wine, and he never let her have a decent

159

bottle of that, even at Christmas. She got a couple of bottles of cheap German Riesling if she was lucky.

As she thought about all this now, a particularly offensive word beginning with "c" came to mind which Kay despised and never uttered. But if anyone ever deserved to be called one, it was Alan.

Going through the hotel bills, she discovered that less than a week after they had returned from Spain, he had spent £769 on two nights in a hotel in London. That was one she was going to have to commit to memory for future use. There were many similar bills.

For the next few minutes, she worked at memorising the dates and locations of several of these hotel stays. The information could come in very useful later on. But what she had was not enough. She needed more – much more.

Chapter Fourteen
February 2018

Alan's regular bank statements did not yield anything untoward. It seemed that he kept his extravagant gestures purely on his credit card, but she did notice something unusual. There were no signs of any payments to the credit card company coming out of his regular current account. But on the credit card she could see that, despite him running up thousands every month, it was regularly being paid off in full.

The question was, where had he been getting the money from to pay it? He earned a good salary from his high-flying retail job, but there was no way it was enough to cover the sorts of sums he was splashing around, and he wasn't using his wages for that anyway. The answer had to be here somewhere and Kay was determined to find it.

She delved further into the folder, and soon found what she was looking for. Tucked away at the back of his regular bank statements were some additional statements from a bank, the name of which she was unfamiliar with. The logo, however, did ring a bell in her head. It was a picture of a tiger with a mountain in the background. Where had she seen that image before?

Two things leapt out at her from the statement. Firstly, the address of the bank was in Switzerland. Banks in that country had a reputation for being safe havens where people could salt away money they wanted to hide.

Secondly, the balance on the account was over €300,000.

She was astounded. How had he acquired such a sum? She scanned through the statements. There were several credits over the past two years going through to the account, all from the same source and all for roughly the same amount, approximately €50,000 each time. She could also see that it was from this account that he had been paying his credit card bills.

All of the payments into the account were from a name she recognised. It was a major wine producer in France, one that she knew her husband dealt with. He had negotiated a major deal worth millions of pounds with the company only a year or two before.

Kay thought back to the rumours that had been circulating about her husband's employers. A series of poor results had led to accusations of financial mismanagement in the City as the share price had plummeted.

Could it be that the mismanagement stretched to fraud? It was pretty obvious to Kay what was going on here. He had negotiated a favourable deal for the supplier and they were giving him backhanders in return. What's more, it seemed like he was getting away with it. With nothing going through his company's books, there would be no trail of money leading back to him.

It was only February now. A further ten months had passed since then, and as far as she knew, he was still securely in his job, despite the internal investigations going on. But then he was a senior manager. She knew that years before he was always pulling little stunts to fiddle on expenses here and there. He had said at the time that, as he was a senior and respected manager, no one would ever dare question him, and besides, it was all perks of the job.

It looked as if his dishonesty had now spread way beyond a few inflated mileage claims. He was on the fiddle in a big way, without a doubt, and it wouldn't surprise her if Lucy was in on it as well. She worked in the accounts department, just as Kay had years ago, and she remembered how he used to get her to push things through that others might have red-flagged.

The bank statement contained both the sort code and the account number of his bank in Switzerland. Looking at the picture of the tiger again, she suddenly remembered where she had seen it before. It had been earlier this morning when she was rummaging through the mess in his drawer.

She crossed back over to the desk and opened the drawer again. Inside was a small, black, plastic device with an LCD strip on it, no bigger than a credit card. She had originally mistaken it for a calculator, but when she remembered that the logo on it matched the one on the bank statement, she realised what it must be.

Quickly she turned her attention back to the laptop and flicked through his bookmarks. Finding a link to the bank, she clicked on it, taking her straight to the login screen for online banking. She was pleased to see that the online banking ID, different from the account number on the statement, was already waiting in the login box for her.

Allowing his web browser to remember all his IDs and passwords so he didn't have to fill them in each time was yet another example of lax security. He was handing all of this to her on a plate.

She attempted to log on, wondering if she could get through security as she had before. Two security questions came up. The first asked for the name of his favourite sports team. That was easy. He was always banging on about Chelsea which all went straight over Kay's head. She was not remotely interested in football, preferring motor racing, something that Alan had dismissed as "sad tossers driving around in circles".

The second was that old favourite, his mother's maiden name. She knew that, too, because his parents had got divorced not long after Kay and Alan had married. At the time, his mother had made a big thing of going back to her maiden name, insisting it be prefixed with 'Ms'.

The final hurdle was using the security key. She had something similar for her own bank and knew she would have to put a passcode into it. She switched it on and found it was asking her for a six-digit code. He couldn't have been stupid enough to use his date of birth again, could he? She typed in 251064.

It worked – he really had been that stupid. All she had to do now was type in the new code which had flashed up on the device.

It was as simple as that and now she was sitting there in front of her husband's illicit account, looking at over €300,000, which by her calculations must amount to at least a quarter of a million pounds. And this was ten months ago. How much more had he added since?

What should she do now? She could steal the money. Why not? She was in Universe 2.0. What was the worst that could happen? It would be worth doing it, just to see if she could get away with it without any consequences. If all went smoothly, she could do it all again once she got back into the real world. Yes, this was a good idea. She would have a consequence-free dress rehearsal.

She clicked on the button marked "Make a payment" and then filled in the section marked "Create a payee". She put in her name and current account details. Then she entered the entire balance as the amount.

Just before she hit send, an amusing thought occurred to her. While she was here, she might as well have a little fun and make the Alan of this universe squirm. She would derive a lot of satisfaction from that.

She reduced the amount in the transfer box by eight euros, which would leave that as the remaining balance on the account. She chuckled as she did so, looking forward to telling him exactly why she had left him with that exact amount. Then she hit send, wondering if such a huge transaction would go through undetected.

It went through without a hitch and a confirmation appeared on the screen. Kay was amazed. Were amounts that large not questioned when they were moved around? She was sure they would be in England. Perhaps that was not the case with Swiss bank accounts. There were all sorts of rich, not to mention corrupt, people using them to move around millions. Her six-figure sum probably wasn't enough to even bat an electronic eyelid.

The next thing to check was whether or not it had reached her account safely. Logging onto her online banking through her mobile phone, she was delighted to see the full amount sitting in her current account. Mission accomplished!

Relaxing for a moment, she felt a rumble in her stomach as her brain informed her she was hungry. Checking her watch, she discovered it was already past lunchtime. She had been at this for over three hours and she needed to eat. But before that, she needed to memorise as much as possible of what she had seen if she was going to be able to use this information again in the future.

She began with his Swiss bank account. It had a five-digit sort code and a twelve-digit account number. Over and over she spoke them out loud, as well as writing them down twenty times on a piece of paper. She remembered being told at school that this helped permanently etch a number into one's brain.

Next, she memorised the dates of the transactions from the wine company into the account. She would need this information for what she had in mind. It was essential if Alan

166

was to believe she knew everything when she came to confront him over it.

Satisfied she had done all she could, she left his office, not bothering to cover her tracks behind her. There was no need. She headed downstairs, made herself a quick sandwich, then pulled on her coat and headed into town.

She stopped at the cashpoint, drew out as much cash as she could and then, on a whim, made for the taxi rank. When she asked the taxi driver to take her to London, he couldn't believe his luck. Such fares didn't come up too often, she imagined.

The taxi cost her £150 and he insisted on payment in advance, but she wasn't bothered about the cost. She had achieved what she had come here to do today and didn't intend to hang around the house watching *Bridget Jones's Diary* like she had the first time around on Valentine's Day. She was going to live the life of Riley instead.

While she was in the taxi, she took great pleasure in texting Alan:

You might want to check the balance of your secret account. Don't worry, it hasn't all gone. There's enough left for you to get yourself an omelette next time you're in Marbella.

A few minutes later, her phone rang and his name flashed up. She could have answered but found it more satisfying to simply press reject instead. Shortly after that, she got a notification that had received a voicemail. She ignored that as well. Then the texts started coming, first anger, then pleading and bargaining. At this point, she switched her phone off. Let him sweat.

In London, she headed straight for Oxford Street where she blew several hundred on a complete outfit for the evening. Then she headed for a swanky hotel in Mayfair. Paying for their best room upfront and leaving her credit card at reception, she pretty much had carte blanche to spend what she liked.

She took full advantage of the hotel's spa and beauty facilities. She had a massage from a very fit, young man, then a full makeover and a hairdo. By the evening, when she was ready to go out, she looked amazing, as she admired herself in the full-length red dress she had bought earlier. It also helped that, at this time, she still had all her teeth.

Kay knew that finding a restaurant to eat at on Valentine's Day would be difficult, so she had an early dinner at the hotel and then headed out to Covent Garden. It was a place she had loved going to with friends in her youth but had not had the chance to visit since getting married.

It was just as vibrant and exciting as she remembered, and she was free to enjoy it as she pleased. It was quite mild for a February evening, and she did not feel in the slightest bit cold, even with only the light jacket she was wearing over her dress.

She was surrounded by people enjoying themselves as she walked through the streets, revelling in the atmosphere.

Finding a lively bar, she ordered herself a White Russian and sat down at the bar, feeling confident and happy. It was amazing what difference a change of scene and a little pampering could do. She was unrecognisable from the bedraggled hag who would be frequenting The Red Lion just a few months later.

All evening, men came over to chat her up. They were not sad desperadoes like those she had taken home to her flat for joyless sex these past months, but well-groomed, intelligent, professional men.

This all showed that she still had it. The attention was a massive ego booster for Kay. It had been one thing revelling in the joy of two days back in her teenage body, but here she was, in her forties, and she could still be a hot prospect if she put her mind to it. All she had to do in the future was look after herself properly and she could have a new lease of life. A new set of teeth would also come in handy. With the money that would hopefully be coming her way, that would be her priority.

Late in the evening, she met a man she felt a real affinity with. He was around her age and when they got chatting, she discovered he was local to where she lived. His name was Robert and he worked as a designer for a Grand Prix team based not far from Oxford. He was down in London for the official launch of his team's new car for the forthcoming season.

Kay was a lifelong fan of Formula One, so they had plenty to talk about. She was able to make very encouraging noises about his team's prospects for the year ahead, knowing already that they were going to win both the driver's and constructor's championships.

She enjoyed his company more than she had any man's for a long time, with the possible exception of Kent. She knew that it could go no further, at least in this universe, but that didn't rule out the possibility of seeing him again when she made it back to her own.

Having made a solid investment in her financial future today, maybe here was a chance to make an investment of a personal nature. She needed to find out as much as she could about him, so she could look him up again in the future. He wouldn't remember this meeting, but she was sure she could engineer another encounter.

By the end of the evening, she knew where he worked, where he lived, and where he liked to spend his free time. There was a slight element of stalking behaviour about what she was doing, but it could be forgiven under the circumstances.

As far as tonight went, she had an ideal opportunity to take him for a test drive. Turning the conversation to personal matters, she made sure she asked him enough questions to ensure that he wasn't married. She wasn't making that mistake again. But when she asked him if he would like to come back to her hotel, she was in for a surprise.

He politely declined the offer. That hadn't been something she had been expecting. He explained he would prefer to get to know her better first and asked if they could meet up for a dinner date once they were back in Oxford.

He wasn't just brushing her off; she could see how keen he was to see her again. Perhaps for once, she had found herself a decent man. It made a refreshing change, as there didn't seem to be many like him around these days.

Being a gentleman, he escorted her back to her hotel and kissed her goodnight at the door, with a promise that they would see each other again soon. For this Robert, sadly, it would never happen. From Kay's perspective, all she had to hope now was that the version of him in her own universe would still be available ten months later. He was a pretty decent catch and it would be no surprise if he got snapped up in the interim.

Content with her day's work, she drifted off to sleep in the luxurious surroundings of her penthouse suite, looking forward to the next day. If all went as planned, it was going to be a day to savour.

Chapter Fifteen
December 2018

It was Christmas Eve, and Kay was back in front of the mirror, discussing her latest trip with the angel.

"I'm impressed," said the angel. "You've made excellent use of your time there in a way very few people doing this ever have. If I were a teacher I'd be giving you an A+. Now I'm looking forward to seeing how you use the knowledge you've gained."

"Well, keep watching," replied Kay. "But haven't you already delved into my thoughts to see what's on the cards?"

"I don't read every thought," replied the angel. "If I did that, it would be like watching a football match when I already knew the result. I could just as easily nip into the future to see what you do next, but haven't done that either. I find this all a lot more entertaining if I avoid spoilers."

"Good, well, all I can say is enjoy," replied Kay. "I've got some big plans lined up for today. And now I must get on, but before you go, there is one thing I need to ask."

"Ask away," replied her younger image.

"If I'm not here tomorrow, can you come and find me? By that I mean not in this flat, but somewhere else. I will make sure I am somewhere where there is a mirror."

"That's not a problem," said the angel. "I will see you then."

Left alone, Kay considered her options. She was due in work at 9am but took an executive decision to give it a miss. This was a risk. If her plans did not come to fruition, she could find herself worse off than before. Failing to turn up at work on a busy Christmas Eve was highly likely to be a sackable offence.

No matter, she would have to take the gamble. There was no way she was waiting another day, not with McVie threatening to cut her electricity off. She also needed to act while the information was as fresh as possible in her mind. It might be a good idea if she got as much of it down on paper now as she could, as even a few hours could make all the difference.

She rummaged in her bag, looking for a pen and something to write on. Finding a pen wasn't a problem, but she ended up having to tear open an empty cigarette packet so she could write on the inside.

She prayed her memory wouldn't let her down. Thankfully it seemed that the repetitive action of writing down the numbers twenty times had worked. She was reasonably confident she had got the account number, sort code, and the dates the money had been transferred correct. This would surely be enough. Anything else she could remember on top of that would be a bonus.

She checked her phone next, ensuring she had the home number of Alan's boss, Nigel. Kay and Alan had had dinner with him and his wife a few times, requiring Kay to speak with her a few times to make the arrangements. She might need that number later, as it formed part of the slightly altered plan she had formed the previous afternoon.

While she had been enjoying her massage in the hotel, Kay had thought in great detail about how best to utilise the information she had found. Her initial plan had been to replicate what she had done before and just transfer the money out of his account and into hers. However, the more she thought about this, the more she realised it wasn't a very realistic or sensible option.

Firstly, she had to be in the house to do it, as she couldn't access the account without the passcode key he kept in his desk. And she couldn't get in the house easily due to the changed locks. Potentially she could break in, it was still her house after all, but even if she managed to do all that undetected, then there was another pitfall.

The money had clearly been fraudulently obtained, so transferring it all into her account was a bad idea. If Alan's crimes were later exposed, she would look just as guilty as him. The money would be confiscated at the very least and in a worst-case scenario she could end up in prison. There was no way she was risking doing time for his crimes. She couldn't touch a penny of his dirty money.

174

Shelving that idea, she soon began to formulate an alternative plan. It was audacious, but her successes to date had left her brimful of confidence.

With a clear battle plan in place, she got ready quickly and headed out. Before she did so, she took the time to phone work to tell them she wasn't coming in, claiming she had the flu. She was pretty sure they didn't believe her, but she had to go through the motions, just in case today didn't work out.

If all went well, it wouldn't matter. She wouldn't need the job any longer and she still had her pay for the current month to come. Most of her wages would have gone to McVie for the rent she already owed and next month's, but she had no intention whatsoever of giving him a penny of it. She wouldn't be living there any longer after today.

She walked briskly in the frosty air, taking a detour to avoid the town centre. As an added precaution, she put her hood up. She didn't want to be seen by anyone from work, as they would be bound to grass her up.

It had been several months since she had last visited her marital home and when she arrived she was dismayed to see the state of the garden. Her well-kept front lawn was scruffy and unkempt. The borders were messy and full of weeds. It was obvious no one had bothered with it since Kay had left.

There were two cars on the drive: Alan's company Mercedes, which she recognised, and a red Toyota which she didn't. Presumably that belonged to Lucy. That meant they were probably both in, which pleased Kay. She would get double the satisfaction from dropping her bombshell on both of them at the same time.

She walked up the path to the front door and rang the doorbell. A few seconds later, Lucy answered with a thick, navy dressing gown wrapped around her, ginger curls cascading around her shoulders. She was taken aback to see Kay and momentarily lost for words.

"Is Alan in, please?" asked Kay, seizing the initiative.

"Alan!" yelled Lucy. "It's for you."

"Who is it?" called Alan, from the kitchen, over the sound of the radio.

"You'd better come and see," called Lucy, throwing a dirty look at their visitor. "Wait here," she said to Kay, closing the door behind her.

Lucy had looked somewhat uncomfortable, Kay thought. Good. Kay was probably the last person she had expected to see. You could never underestimate the element of surprise. On the few occasions the two of them had crossed paths previously, Lucy had been quite vile towards her. This morning, caught off guard, perhaps she would be vulnerable.

The door opened and Alan appeared, wearing a dressing gown that matched Lucy's. Unsurprisingly, he looked none too pleased to see her.

"What are you doing here, Kay?" he snapped. "I told you to stay away."

"Season's greetings to you, too," said Kay, breezily. "I'm here because we have some things to discuss. Aren't you going to invite me in?"

"No, I'm bloody not," he replied. "Anything you want to say to me, you can say through my solicitor. Now if you don't mind, it's Christmas Eve and Lucy and I have got plans. Good day."

He went to close the door, but before he could, Kay said, "Just let me say five words, and if you don't want to hear what I've got to say after you've heard them, I'll go."

"Go on, then, five words," said Alan. "And then you can clear off."

"Zurich Tiger Swiss bank account," said Kay, taking her time over the words, emphasising each one in turn.

She watched, delighted, as the colour drained from his face.

"I don't know what you're talking about," he blustered.

"Oh, I think you do. I know all about it," said Kay. "I suppose you thought you were being clever, hiding it from me. Didn't you?"

"If such an account does exist, it's my money," he said defensively. "I earned it fair and square. So don't even think about trying to get a cut in the divorce settlement."

"Fair and square, eh?" asked Kay. "You know I don't think it's just me that you've been hiding this account from, because I know where that money came from. Remember that deal you struck with that major vineyard in France? I know all about it. I think you've been a bit of a naughty boy, haven't you?"

Kay was enjoying this immensely.

"Now, are you sure you don't want to invite me in?" she added. "Is that coffee I can smell on the go?"

"Whatever you think you know it's all above board," he said, clearly floundering with a look of guilt written all over his face. "You've got nothing on me."

"Well, if that's the case, you won't mind me ringing Nigel to confirm that," she said, holding up her mobile phone. "Look, I've got his number on my phone right here."

She went as if to dial, but before she pressed the button he hurriedly said, "No, don't do that. You'd better come in and we can talk about it."

"That's better," said Kay.

He looked terrified, like a naughty schoolboy, caught red-handed and sent to the headmaster for punishment. And so he should. Kay now had him exactly where she wanted him.

He led her through to the kitchen, where the coffee pot was brewing and the radio was playing "Fairytale of New

York". The place was a picture of domestic bliss. At least she keeps the house tidier than the garden, thought Kay.

Having recovered from her initial element of surprise, Lucy was returning to her normal bitchy self, a look of utter contempt on her face as she saw Kay enter the room.

"What have you let this old slapper in for?" she said to Alan. "I don't want her in here, spoiling our Christmas."

Looking Kay straight in the eye, she added, "Sorry, love, it's Christmas Eve and there's no room at the inn." She looked pleased as pie with this remark, smirking at Kay from her cruel little face.

"Shut up a minute, Lucy," said Alan, moving over to join her. "This is serious."

Kay couldn't help but smile, looking at the two of them in their matching his and hers towelling robes. Her smile didn't go unnoticed by Lucy.

"Oh my God, look at her teeth!" exclaimed Lucy, who hadn't seen Kay since the incident that had caused their unfortunate removal. "You skanky cow!"

Kay didn't mind the insult. It would just make what she was going to deliver in return that much sweeter.

"Little girl, you should listen to your sugar daddy here and shut up," replied Kay. "Not that there is going to be much sugar coming your way in the near future, I fear."

Lucy remained silent but fixed Kay with an evil glare.

"Come on, then, out with it," said Alan. "Let's get this over with. What do you want?"

"Well, as I said at the door, I know all about your secret Swiss bank account."

"So you say," said Alan, "but you could be bluffing for all I know. If you think you've got something on me, then let's see the evidence."

"Oh I've got plenty," said Kay. "Let me spell out the details."

And she did just that, giving him the account number, sort code, and the dates and amounts of the transactions.

"And just in case you were wondering, I have copies of all the documents safely tucked away," she said. This was a lie, but he had no way of knowing that. "I'm quite sure that Nigel would be very interested to see them, what with all the rumours going around about financial irregularities. Don't you agree, Lucy? You do work in the accounts department, after all."

It was clear from the guilty look on Lucy's face that she knew all about this. It was as she had suspected all along. The two of them were in it together up to their necks.

"Then there are the police, of course. I'm sure they'd be very interested to hear about all of this."

"You fucking idiot!" shouted Lucy, straight at Alan with a look of fury on her face. "You said you'd covered your tracks. How did she find out about this?"

"Yes, how did you find out, Kay?" asked Alan.

"How I found out isn't important," replied Kay. "It's the fact that I have found out that you should be worrying about. And more importantly, what I am going to do about it."

"If you were going to tell the police about this, you already would have," surmised Alan, correctly. "So what are you after – some of the spoils? How about we cut you in?"

"What the fuck?" exclaimed Lucy. "We're not giving this toothless hag any of our money!"

"Do you want to go to prison?" said Alan to Lucy. "Because that's what we could be looking at here. Now just shut up and let me deal with this."

Seeing the two of them turn on each other added nicely to Kay's sense of satisfaction at how well events were proceeding.

Turning back to Kay, Alan asked. "So, how much do you want to keep quiet? Fifty grand? Will that make this all go away?"

"Fifty grand!" exclaimed Lucy. "She'll only waste it on booze and fags. Look at the state of her. What about that Caribbean cruise you promised me?"

"For the last time, Lucy, shut up!" shouted Alan. "And turn that fucking radio off."

Slade had begun belting out their Christmas classic, which was completely inappropriate for the moment. Shocked at being shouted at by Alan like that, Lucy complied and switched it off.

"I don't want your dirty money, Alan," said Kay. "You can keep it. If I touch that I'll be as tainted as you are."

"So what do you want, then?" he asked.

"I want a clean and quick divorce. And I want this house and everything in it, furniture and all. I did buy most of it in the first place, after all. It'll be easy enough to arrange. We've no mortgage and no other complications. You just sign it over to me, and I'll make sure all the evidence of your fraudulent behaviour is destroyed."

"You must be joking," he said. "This house has got to be worth about four hundred grand."

"Well, the last time I looked, you had the best part of that in your dodgy account, so I am sure you won't go hungry."

"You can't expect me to up sticks and leave just like that," he protested.

"Oh I can," said Kay. "I've got you over a barrel and I can do exactly what I want." She walked over to the fridge and opened the door. It was stacked with festive goodies, the highlight being a large turkey crown from M&S.

"That turkey looks lovely," she said appreciatively. "I think I'm going to enjoy that tomorrow," she said.

"You must be joking," said Lucy. "You're not having Christmas dinner here."

"I think you'll find it's you that won't be here," replied Kay. "What was it you said to me earlier? No room at the inn? Well, there's no room at the inn here for you – either of you. You can pack your bags this morning and leave. I said I wanted everything in the house. Well, that includes the food in the fridge as well."

"Haven't you forgotten something?" asked Alan. "What about Maddie? She's driving down from Durham today for Christmas."

"I'm glad you mentioned Maddie because that's another thing," said Kay. "I'm disgusted with the way you've poisoned her mind against me. So you are going to speak to her today and put that right. You are going to tell her I'm not the bad mother you made me out to be and that everything you said to her was fabricated out of spite. I fully expect her to be here tonight and for things to be right between us. If you do that, then I will be happy to add her to the list of people that I am not going to tell about your fraudulent behaviour."

"How are you going to explain to her that you've kicked us out on Christmas Eve?" asked Alan. "That's not going to look very good, is it?"

"Oh that's simple enough," replied Kay. "You're going to do it for me. You just need to tell her that you and Lucy have decided to go away for Christmas and now that the divorce is going through, you've decided to give me back the house as part of the deal. Just make sure it sounds convincing, because don't forget, I've got Nigel's number on speed dial."

"Alan, you're not seriously going to let her do this to us, are you?" asked Lucy. "She can't throw us out like this, can she?"

"I think you'll find she can," said Alan, resignedly.

"But where are we going to go?" replied Lucy, barely able to grasp the reality of the situation.

"Well, I've got a lovely little flat in town you can have," said Kay, barely able to conceal her giggles. "It's got all mod cons, en suite bathroom, the lot. It even has its own in-house restaurant. I recommend the three-day-old fish cakes – a house speciality. And the landlord is a lovely chap, like a real-life Father Christmas."

"It'll be OK, Lucy, we'll get a hotel for tonight," said Alan, ignoring Kay's sarcasm.

"But what about all our stuff?" asked Lucy, looking distraught. Sure enough, she began to cry.

Kay nearly felt sorry for her at that point but willed herself to be strong, remembering how nasty Lucy had been to her when the boot was on the other foot. She had reaped what she had sown.

184

"You can take all your clothes and personal effects today," said Kay. "As for anything else, you can come back after he's signed over the house to me. But everything that was in here before I moved out stays – furniture, TV, you name it. And I'm having that turkey. It won't be any good to you in a hotel, will it? Now I suggest you go and get dressed and start packing, while I make myself a nice cup of coffee with *my* coffee machine."

She had missed her Tassimo machine. It would make a nice change from the budget brand of instant coffee she had been reduced to drinking in her flat.

"You've not heard the last of this!" shouted Lucy at her, as she got up and headed out of the kitchen.

"Oh I think I have!" shouted Kay after her. "Now what was the number of the police again? Ah yes, 999, that was it."

Alan lingered in the kitchen a while longer after Lucy had headed off up the stairs.

"Kay, it doesn't have to be like this. Maybe we can work something out. I do miss you, you know." He walked over towards her, a conciliatory look in his eye. To her horror, she realised he was about to try and put his arms around her.

"Get away from me," she said. "You miss your money is what you mean. Just be thankful you've still got your job and your secret stash of ill-gotten cash. This could have turned out a hell of a lot worse for you. And let me make one thing clear – you and I are finished – full stop. Now I suggest you salvage what dignity you have left and go upstairs and patch things up with her – that's if she still wants you. She looks like a bit of a gold-digger to me."

With a look of total defeat on his face, he turned about heel and followed Lucy up the stairs, while Kay sipped her coffee in triumph. Had she done enough? Should she have pushed for more? No, the house and getting her daughter back would more than suffice. She wouldn't be rolling in money, but her wages were due in and hopefully, she would still have her job. With no rent or mortgage to pay, she should be able to manage, even on minimum wage.

This was just the beginning. She was only forty-three and this was her big chance to start over. For the first time in years, the future was something to look forward to, rather than fear.

Chapter Sixteen
December 1985

When Kay woke up on Christmas morning, all was well with her world.

Alan and Lucy had departed swiftly the previous day, stuffing what they could into three suitcases. Making sure they both handed over their keys, Kay took great pleasure in escorting them from the premises. They were arguing furiously as they left, blaming each other for the unexpected mishap that had befallen them.

They were both as bad as each other as far as Kay was concerned. If they fell out with each other, that suited her just fine, remembering that old expression, divide and conquer. He would be weaker without her to help fight his battles, that was certain.

Once they were gone, Kay set about removing all trace of them from the house.

She bagged up the remainder of their clothes in black bin liners and took them out to the garage. The same went for all of Lucy's make-up and most of the toiletries, though she couldn't resist keeping some of her posh Molton Brown stuff for herself. Alan had never allowed Kay to have expensive toiletries like that, so it was payback time for all his years of penny-pinching.

Once that was done she set to work cleaning the house from top to bottom. The thought of flakes of Lucy's skin and bits of hair all over the house disgusted her, particularly when she discovered the shower tray clogged up with ginger pubes. She didn't even want to think what part of her anatomy they had come from, but she was pretty sure it wasn't her head.

The worst part was changing the bed. It hadn't been done for a while and Kay recoiled at the crusty yellow stains on the sheets, the source of which was obvious. It was a set of sheets that Kay had bought a couple of years before, but she really couldn't face sleeping in them again, even after a boil wash. Stripped off the bed, they went straight into the dustbin, leaving Kay to replace them with a fresh set from the cupboard.

Remarkably, little had changed around the house in the nine months Kay had been away. It didn't look as if Lucy had made the slightest effort to put her own stamp on the place. The vast majority of things, from the curtains to the towels, were just as Kay had left them. It took no time at all for her to settle back in.

At 4pm, just as it was getting dark, she heard a key in the lock and the front door opened. Her daughter was home.

It had been a while since Kay had seen Maddie, and her appearance had changed considerably. She had been going increasingly gothic over the past year or two, but it was still a shock to see her blonde hair dyed jet black, not to mention the tattoos and piercings she was now adorned with.

Things were awkward between them, to begin with. Alan had called her daughter, as per Kay's instructions, but Maddie was still struggling to understand the situation. Over tea and mince pies in the living room, they had a long heart-to-heart about the events of the past year.

Kay was careful not to slag Alan off, even though that was exactly what he had done to her. In her eyes, that was the worst thing any parent could do during an acrimonious divorce. She simply explained the situation as best she could. It transpired that he had done as Kay had asked and admitted to Maddie that the vile stories he had told her were lies. Clearly, he was taking Kay's threat to expose his illegal activities seriously.

Kay decided that it was time she was honest about a few things, too, including the truth about how she had lost her teeth. Yes, she had been foolish and shouldn't have slept with a married man, but when she explained how crushingly lonely she had been, Maddie seemed to understand.

It seemed Kay hadn't been the only one having a hard time of late. Maddie had a few tales of woe to tell about her somewhat underwhelming first term at university. These were problems that she had not felt able to discuss with Alan. Grateful to have her mother back in her life, she explained what had gone wrong for her at Durham.

Maddie had suffered a bad experience with another student who sounded remarkably similar to Glen. It seemed that making bad choices of men was something that Kay had passed down to the next generation. Empathising with her

189

daughter's problems, she shared the story of what had happened in her past, not leaving anything out, including the abortion. Thankfully, in Maddie's case, she hadn't fallen pregnant.

The wedge that Alan had driven between Kay and her daughter continued to melt away as they talked. There were more than a few tears and a little laughter, too. Most importantly, there were hugs. Mother and daughter were reunited at last.

In the evening, Maddie went out to catch up with her old school friends, advising her mother not to wait up. Remembering the boozy Christmas Eve pub crawls of her youth, Kay imagined her daughter wouldn't roll in until the early hours. This gave her a chance to relax and reflect on all she had achieved so far through her travels and where else she might like to go.

She had no intention of going to the pub tonight. She had only just got the house back, and whilst she didn't imagine that Alan might try and return, she wasn't going to risk leaving the place unattended just yet. Besides, she felt tired. The events of recent days had been quite exhausting, and she could do with a quiet night in.

Now that she was back in the comfort of her own home, a night in would be a pleasure, compared to the confines of the cold, lonely flat. Enjoying the luxury of hot water again, she treated herself to a long, hot bath. Lighting some of her candles that were still on the bathroom windowsill, untouched during her long absence from the house, she immersed herself in the water, relishing the warmth.

Soaking in the bubbles, she closed her eyes, indulging herself in a favourite fantasy or two, as she indulged a little of what she liked to refer to as "me time".

After her bath, she sat down in front of the TV and cracked open a bottle of Baileys that Lucy had kindly left in the fridge for her. After coping with the tiny portable in the flat for months, the 50-inch screen seemed enormous. There wasn't anything on it that she particularly wanted to see, it was just the usual festive tripe. Kay was sure that Christmas TV used to be much better when she was younger. She would find out tomorrow.

A programme counting down the greatest Christmas hits of all time provided mild amusement and provoked more than a little nostalgia. Long before midnight, she fell asleep on the sofa. Waking up around 1am, she took herself up to bed, noticing Maddie was not yet home. She quickly fell back into a deep sleep.

Now it was Christmas morning and a low sun was shining into her bedroom window. Getting up, she cast a look outside into the back garden. There was not even a touch of frost to be seen, let alone any snow. So that was another Christmas that had come around without so much as a sniff of the white stuff.

It was almost 9am. She had slept naked the previous night, realising when she got to bed that she had no nightwear.

191

Unlike in the flat, where she had frequently slept in her clothes just to keep warm, it was lovely and warm in the house so she had no problem with sleeping au naturel.

Kay remembered bagging up some nighties when she had done her big clear-out, but they were in the garage. She wouldn't have worn them, anyway. She might have been drinking Lucy's Baileys, and washing her hair with Molton Brown shampoo, but there was no way she was wearing any of the bitch's clothes.

Kay had only the clothes she had arrived in the previous day which meant she was going to have to brave a trip back to the flat. Most of the clothes she had at the flat were old and worn out, but they would have to do for now. She would go out and get herself some new stuff as soon as the shops reopened after Christmas, but for this morning, perhaps she could borrow some clothes from her daughter.

Leaving the bedroom, she walked along the landing, enjoying the luxurious feel of the soft, cream carpet beneath her feet. Opening her daughter's bedroom door, she peeked inside to see that Maddie was dead to the world, still half-dressed and snoring softly on top of her quilt. She looked as if she had crashed out from a skinful the night before and probably wouldn't wake up for hours yet.

Kay crept into the room and managed to find a baggy, black T-shirt, some socks and some underwear. These would do. She took them back to her own room and put them on, along with the pair of jeans she had worn the previous day. She knew there was no way she would have squeezed into a pair of Maddie's, so they would have to do.

Fully dressed, she looked into the full-length mirror on the front of one of the wardrobe doors to see the angel looking back at her. Kay noticed that her reflection was wearing a truly horrible Christmas jumper with reindeer and red lights on it.

"Merry Christmas," said the angel. "Like the outfit?"

"It's hideous," replied Kay.

"Well, you should know," replied the angel. "You wore this on Christmas Day in 1996."

"Don't remind me," said Kay. "Alan bought it for me and insisted I wore it all day. That's one Christmas I'd rather forget."

"Well, I think it's fair to say you're going to have a better one this year," replied the angel. "I imagine it's going to be a lot better than you were expecting before I came along."

"I certainly am," replied Kay. "I'm going to be having double the fun this year. With your help, I'm going to have two Christmas Days."

"I thought as much," replied the angel. "So, where are we off to? I'm guessing it won't be 1996."

"Not, it will not," replied Kay. "I was hoping you might help me pick a year. I want to go back to Christmas Day when I was a child. I can't distinguish one from another, so it's hard to pick a particular year. I would ask for one when there was a proper white Christmas, but I'm pretty sure there has never been one, not one I can remember, anyway."

"It depends what you mean by a proper one," said the angel.

"I mean one when several inches of snow are falling on Christmas morning and you can go out and build a snowman," replied Kay.

"Believe it or not, around here, you would have to go back to 1938 for that. There have been years more recently with the odd sleety shower, or some snow lying on the ground from earlier in the week, but nothing that fits your definition."

"Forget the snow, then," said Kay. "I just want to go back and spend the day with my mum and dad, and maybe my grandparents, too. They all died when I was a teenager, so it needs to be before then, but not too young. I've no desire to find myself wearing nappies. You can see into the depths of my memories, so can you reach inside and pick me out a good year?"

"I think I can," said the angel, browsing through Kay's past Christmas Days, including long-buried memories that Kay would struggle to recall by herself. "How does 1985 sound?"

"I would have been ten," replied Kay. "That sounds perfect. Now, before you go, can I ask you a question?"

"Go ahead," replied the angel.

"It's about the future," said Kay.

"You know the rules. I can't tell you about the future."

"It's only a little thing, to do with what I said earlier about snow at Christmas," replied Kay. "It's just that I am so fed up with year after year watching TV ads and Christmas specials with everything covered in snow, not to mention all the decorations and cards. Then, when Christmas Day comes, there's not a hint of snow this side of the Arctic Circle. I just want to know one thing. In my lifetime, will I ever see a proper white Christmas?"

"Wait until 2029," replied the angel. "You'll have more snow then than you know what to do with."

"Well, that's alright, then," said Kay. "It's something to look forward to."

"You might not say that when the time comes," replied the angel. "Have you ever seen that film *The Day After Tomorrow*?"

"That bad?" asked Kay.

"Yes, that bad," replied the angel. "Still, don't worry about that for now. It's a long way off, just be prepared when the time comes. As for today, a return trip to 1985, wasn't it?"

"It certainly was," replied Kay. "Let's get going."

She swiftly found herself back in her childhood room, the same one she had recently woken up in aged eighteen. It had been summer then, but this time the room was dark, only the ladybird nightlight that had comforted her as a small child casting any light into the gloom.

Getting out of bed, she opened the curtains to see that it was still semi-dark outside. Her bedroom at the back of the house looked out across the playing fields where she had spent so many happy hours as a kid. The skies were clear and there was an orange glow on the horizon illuminating the branches of the trees which stood starkly, devoid of leaves, on the far side of the park. Sunrise was still several minutes away.

A single bright star, or maybe a planet, was still visible glowing brightly just above the trees in the semi-dark skies. It brought to mind the Star of Bethlehem.

She crossed to the switch by the door and flicked it on, lighting up her room which was quite different to the last time she had seen it. Now at an earlier stage of its evolution, the posters on the wall were pin-ups from Smash Hits of Duran Duran and Wham! The centrepiece was of A-ha, triggering memories from Kay of her first crush on Morten Harket.

The room was full of toys and books, which she couldn't resist browsing through. Enid Blyton featured heavily on her bookshelves and she remembered how eagerly she had devoured *The Famous Five* and *Malory Towers* series at around this age. She picked one of the books now and began to flick through it.

Distracted by the unmistakable clink of coffee cups from the kitchen, she rushed downstairs, eager to see her parents. An hour later, after a family breakfast of bacon and eggs, the three of them were sitting under the Christmas tree opening their presents.

Despite the fact she had been here before, Kay's presents were still a surprise to her. She couldn't remember exactly what presents she had got in which year and was able to guess very few from the shapes.

From My Little Pony to Spirograph, each one she opened brought back a special memory of its own. The delight on her face was possibly greater than it had been the first time around. It was the sheer nostalgic joy of it all that was filling her with happiness. The look was not lost on her parents, just as happy as she was as they watched their little girl's face light up.

While Mum cooked dinner, she and Dad played Mouse Trap, another new present. It seemed a lot more solid than the modern version she had bought more recently for her daughter. A lot of things had been redesigned over the years, thought Kay, and not always for the better. You couldn't beat the classic designs.

When Dad headed off to the pub at midday for a Christmas drink, Kay flicked on the TV to find the bearded face of a youthful-looking Noel Edmonds grinning back at her from on top of the BT Tower. She wasn't Edmonds' biggest fan, but the nostalgia factor was compensation on this occasion, particularly when The Krankies appeared.

At 12.30pm her maternal grandparents arrived, two people very dear to her. She had loved visiting their big, old house in Yorkshire as a kid, with its roaring, open fireplace and outside toilet which froze over in the winter. They brought more presents, including Monopoly, which her grandfather claimed to be world champion at.

Dinner was meant to be at 1pm, but her dad's tardy return from the pub meant that it was another half an hour before they were all sitting down around the table. The food was delicious, as her mother's cooking always had been. She had a special way of making the roast potatoes extra crispy that no one else had ever bettered, including Kay herself. She must ask her the secret while she had the chance.

Throughout the meal, everyone was joking and laughing, even at the awful cracker jokes which were one of those things, like air travel, which seemed unchanged by the passing of time. Kay made sure she savoured every mouthful of food and every moment of conversation while she was at the table, appreciating how lucky she was to be seeing these special people again this one last time.

By a quarter to three, they had all repaired to the living room in preparation for The Queen's Speech. When her father switched the TV back on, she was able to catch the last few minutes of the annual Christmas edition of *Top of the Pops*, where Wham! were performing "I'm Your Man".

"Ooh, I like him," said her grandmother about George Michael. "Hasn't he got lovely teeth?"

Kay had liked him, too; more than that, she had adored him. He had been her first crush, at the age of nine. It made no difference when his true sexuality was revealed many years later – her adoration never faded.

Now she was reminded of another Christmas Day, only a couple of years ago, when she had learnt of George's death. It had been at the end of a year when The Grim Reaper had taken more than his fair share of the pop icons Kay had grown up with. The loss of George had hit her more than any of the others. It was as if part of her childhood had been taken away forever. Alan hadn't cared, but then he never did, scoffing at her grief, saying she had never met him so why should she care? He never understood anything.

After The Queen's Speech, her grandfather asked to turn over to ITV to watch the Bond film, then promptly fell asleep during the opening credits. While he snored away, Kay played gin rummy for pennies with her grandmother, who according to her had been a bit of a legend at the card tables in her younger days. She couldn't have been that great because Kay always won, though she suspected that her grandmother let her.

At teatime, her mother put on a fabulous spread of cold cuts, pastries and other nibbles. It was way more food than five people could eat, but people always over-catered at Christmas. With no shops open again until the 27th, she had ensured that there would be plenty of food to keep the family going.

Kay took full advantage. This was one of the only occasions in her life when she could feast to her heart's content and not have to worry about the consequences for her waistline. This didn't go unnoticed by the family.

"By heck, your lass has got a good appetite on her," remarked her grandfather, as Kay wolfed down the pork pies and slices of her mother's delicious home-baked honey roast ham.

Later they played charades and then watched the *Only Fools and Horses* Christmas special, leading her to conclude that Christmas TV really had been better in the past.

The day had been pretty much perfect in every respect. The angel had picked a good year. By 9pm she was ready for bed, but Christmas was not yet over. She would get to do it all over again tomorrow.

Chapter Seventeen
December 2018

Back in the present day, Kay took her leave of the angel quickly. Not only did she have a Christmas dinner to cook, but she also had to go out and get back before Maddie woke up. She had bought her daughter a Christmas present but had left it in the flat.

It was mild and cloudy outside, not at all festive, but quite pleasant to be walking in compared to the cold of recent days. There was something special about going out for a walk on Christmas morning. It was different from any other day of the year. You could guarantee everyone you met, from kids to dog walkers, would greet you with a cheery smile and a "Merry Christmas".

She still wished there was snow, though. Never mind, only another eleven years to wait, according to the angel.

From the new estate, the quickest way to the flat was across the park, the same one where she had lost her virginity to Glen on the night of the summer ball all those years ago. Normally it was a quiet place, but today something was going on. At the far side of the park, just past the children's playground, was a wooded area where she normally cut through the trees. This route brought her out onto the main road, only a few minutes walk from the chip shop.

As Kay got closer she could see the whole wooded area was sealed off with police tape, warning people not to cross. There were several police officers there. It looked as if there had been some major incident. Swerving past the woods, and diverting further up the park, she reached the main road about a hundred yards further up than she usually did, via the park's main entrance.

As she walked down the road towards town she could see several police officers and vehicles around the area. She also recognised Seema Mistry, a local news reporter, with a crew at the scene. It must be something big if it had brought her out on Christmas morning.

The pavement where the path came out of the woods was sealed off, too, and a young policeman directed her to the other side of the road.

"What's going on here?" she asked him.

"I'm not at liberty to say, madam," he said. "But we need to keep this area clear. Please cross to the other pavement and keep walking."

"Merry Christmas to you, too," replied Kay, and crossed to the other side of the road. She would be coming back this way after she had been to the flat. Maybe she could find a more forthcoming policeman who would tell her more then.

The chip shop was deserted, as she had hoped it would be. It was also a complete mess, chip papers strewn everywhere and empty beer bottles and litter all over the floor. It was often a mess on weekend mornings, but never this bad. The townsfolk had clearly had a good party last night.

She let herself in and made her way up to the flat. It was dark and dingy inside, leading her to reach instinctively for the light switch, but nothing happened. The same went for the light switch in the bathroom. It seemed McVie had made good on his promise to cut her electricity off.

No matter, she would never have to see the inside of this hovel again after this morning. She reached under the bed and pulled out the battered suitcase that had been there since the day she moved in, preparing to stuff what meagre belongings she wanted to keep into it.

The bottom drawer of the chest of drawers came off in her hand as she opened it, not for the first time. Inside, she found the necklace she had bought for Maddie, several weeks before. She hadn't wrapped it up, not having known until yesterday if she was even going to see her over Christmas. No matter, there was still time when she got back to the house. There must be some wrapping paper there somewhere.

As for the creaky furniture, cheap portable TV and the rest of the crap in the flat, she decided to abandon it. In the end, all she ended up taking was a few toiletries and half her clothes, abandoning the rest. They weren't even worth bagging up for a charity shop, the state they were in. As far as she was concerned, this wasn't her problem anymore. McVie could deal with it.

As she left the flat for what she hoped would be the last time, she felt like she had just ticked off another box on her quest for salvation. She was free of the dump at last! Or so she thought. Unknown to her, circumstances would bring her back to the flat again sooner than she expected.

She was halfway dragging her suitcase across the chip shop floor when her mobile rang in her handbag. This caught her by surprise. Her mobile hadn't exactly been ringing off the hook recently.

She fumbled quickly in her bag, desperate to get to the phone before it clicked over to voicemail. Grabbing hold of it, she was surprised to see who was calling. It was Kent.

"Hello," she said, "and Merry Christmas!"

Kent didn't return her greeting, a sense of urgency in his voice as he said, "Have you seen the news?"

"No," replied Kay. "Why? What's happened?"

"There's been another murder," replied Kent. "Right here in town. The Christmas Killer has struck again."

"So that's what all the police and reporters were about," said Kay. "I saw them earlier up by the park."

"Yes, that's where it happened," replied Kent. "I'm watching it on telly right now. Can you switch the TV on?"

"I'm not at home," replied Kay. There was the telly in the flat but she wasn't going back up there, and in any case, the electricity had been cut off.

"Well, I'm watching it and it looks pretty grisly. Another young girl apparently – raped and murdered on the woody path last night. Speaking of which, where were you last night? I thought you would have been down the pub."

"I decided to have a quiet night in," replied Kay. "I'll explain more later."

"Well, that brings me to the purpose of my call," said Kent. "I need to see you later – can we meet?"

"Are you sure that's a good idea?" asked Kay. "I'm sure your wife won't be too pleased with you leaving her at home on Christmas Day. Can it wait until tomorrow?"

Much as she would enjoy spending some more time with Kent, Kay had already planned to spend the day at home with her daughter.

"It can't wait until tomorrow," replied Kent. "It's about the murders. I know how we – or rather, you – can solve them. If we leave it another day, someone else could die."

It wasn't difficult to work out what he had in mind.

"I see where you're coming from," replied Kay. "Listen, I need to get back home now. I've already taken my trip back in time for today, so we can't do any more until the morning. Let me think about it, and we'll try and have a get-together and a proper chat later."

"OK," replied Kent. "Craig said he's opening the pub for a couple of hours tonight, just for the regulars. Can you get down there, then?"

"I'll see what I can do," replied Kay. "Speak later."

It was obvious that he was going to ask her to go back in time to unmask the murderer. She was going to have to go back past the scene of the crime to get home, so it would be a good time to try and see what more she could find out. Walking back up the road, she double-checked exactly where the incident had taken place. Quite clearly it had been somewhere on the woody path between the road and the park.

She tried speaking to another policeman at the scene but was met with the same stony-faced, tight-lipped response as before. She would be better off putting the news on at home.

When she got back, it was past 11am but Maddie was still asleep. Kay really ought to get started on the dinner but her mind was now preoccupied with the murder. She had to find out more.

Watching the rolling news coverage in the living room didn't do much to add to what she already knew. The attack had taken place exactly where she expected, sometime the previous night, but they didn't seem to know exactly when. The body had not been discovered until a dog walker had found it after first light. The victim had not yet been formally identified, but the news did state that it fitted the pattern of the other murders. That meant that it would have been a young girl, in her late teens or early twenties.

She continued to watch the coverage as she wrapped Maddie's present with some leftover wrapping paper she found behind the Christmas tree. When she had finished she added her present to the pile underneath the tree. Alan and Lucy had taken the presents they had bought for each other the previous day but had left some for Maddie.

Kay's didn't look like much compared to what Alan had probably spent, especially with his huge pot of dirty cash to draw on, but it would have to do for now. He had always spoiled his daughter rotten at Christmas, whilst Kay's presents from him had steadily declined over the years, both in value and how much thought had gone into them. If she recalled correctly, last year his generosity had extended to a new iron and a tub of Quality Street.

No matter, Kay would treat Maddie to something special after Christmas when she had her finances properly sorted.

She turned the volume up on the TV and headed back to the kitchen to start the cooking. Kay loved cooking roasts and the Christmas dinner was the best of all, especially this year, because everything she needed was there in the fridge and the cupboard, right down to the cranberry sauce. Sorting through it all, she could see that Alan and Lucy had really splashed out. It was all top-quality stuff, mostly from Marks & Spencer.

So much for only shopping at the retailer he worked for. There were hundreds of pounds worth of food and drink in the house. He had never spent this much on Christmas when Kay had been with him. It seemed that he was generous to a T with almost everyone except his wife. That was what made eating the Christmas food he had bought to impress Lucy so satisfying. Today was well and truly payback time.

She wondered where he and Lucy would be spending their Christmas Day. Well, wherever it was, she wasn't going to allow herself to feel sorry for them. They had brought their current situation upon themselves.

As she was peeling spuds, a sleepy and hungover-looking Maddie appeared at the kitchen door.

"What have you got the telly on so loud for?" she complained. "My head hurts."

"I'm not surprised," said Kay. "Sit yourself down and I'll make you some coffee – and Merry Christmas, by the way!"

Kay went back through to the living room to turn the TV off. It had moved on to sports news now, something about Boxing Day football fixtures, a subject in which she had no interest. Just as she pressed the button on the remote, a chilling thought went through her. The dead girl could have been Maddie.

She offered a silent prayer of thanks that her daughter had got home safe and sound and rushed back through to the kitchen, taking Maddie by surprise by giving her a huge hug.

"What was that for?" asked her bemused daughter.

"Did you hear what was on the news before?" asked Kay.

"I wasn't taking a lot of notice," replied Maddie. "Head's throbbing too much."

"There's been a murder in town. That's why I hugged you. I'm just glad you're safe and sound. How did you get home last night?"

"I'm fairly sure I shared a taxi with a couple of people from the pub," she replied, "but the details are a bit vague."

"Thank goodness you did," said Kay. She had banged on at Maddie over and over again about making sure she got home safely and she was glad it had sunk in. She then proceeded to tell her more about the recent spate of murders.

It all came as quite a shock to Maddie who, having been up in Durham, caught up in the student Christmas party circuit, had been completely unaware of the murders going on in Oxfordshire.

"Why didn't you warn me about this last night?" asked Maddie. "And how come no one said anything about it in the pub?"

"Well, the first two murders were in Oxford and Kidlington," replied Kay. "You know what it's like in this town. No one takes any notice of anything unless it's right under their noses. Most of the time they're too busy gossiping about each other's sex lives. Plus, nothing big like this ever happens here, does it? I can't ever remember a murder in this town before."

"Do they know who was killed?" asked Maddie.

"A young woman is all they are saying," said Kay. "The last two were both in their late teens."

"God, I hope it's not one of my friends," replied Maddie.

"Well, let's try not to think about it for now," said Kay. "There's no point speculating until we know more. Now you're up, you can help me with the dinner."

The turkey crown went down a treat. Over lunch, they shared a bottle of champagne that Alan had kindly left in the fridge for them. It was Moët & Chandon, rather than the supermarket brand that he usually bought. Later they went through to the living room and opened presents.

"I'm sorry it's not much," said Kay. "Things have been a little fraught recently, as you know. But I'll make it up to you."

"Don't worry, I love it," replied Maddie, as she placed the silver chain around her neck.

Maddie proceeded to open her other presents, the ones Alan had left for her. They were predictably extravagant: a cashmere scarf, the latest iPad and some fancy Belgian chocolates. There was also an expensive-looking gold bracelet, which Kay noted that she did not put on, placing it back in the box. He didn't know his daughter as well as she did. She only ever wore silver jewellery, never gold.

Just after she opened her last present, Maddie's mobile rang.

"It's Dad," said Maddie, answering.

Alan had rung to wish his daughter a happy Christmas, something that Kay could hardly begrudge him. However, there was more to the call than just that.

"Mum, Dad's spending Christmas with Lucy at The Oxfordshire," said Kay. "He's asked if it's OK for me to go over there this evening and spend some time with them."

He had managed to find a pretty decent room at the inn, then, thought Kay. The two of them had spent a very happy wedding anniversary weekend at that hotel many years before. How had he managed to get in there on Christmas Eve?

Perhaps people didn't stay in hotels much at Christmas, she mused. It was a family time, after all. Whatever the reason, he certainly wasn't roughing it. He was probably trying desperately to keep hold of Lucy, worried that she would dump him in his reduced circumstances.

Kay's first instinct was to say no, but then she thought about her chat with Kent earlier. Perhaps it was better if Maddie was out of the way for a while.

"Let me speak to him," said Kay.

Leaving Alan in no doubt that she was doing him a favour, Kay said she had no objection to Maddie joining him and Lucy at the hotel, as long as he came and picked her up and brought her back the next day.

It was dark by the time Alan came for Maddie. Kay didn't let him into the house, not wanting any aggravation with her daughter present. Once they were gone, she turned her attention back to the murder.

She switched the television back on. It was almost five o'clock, and the channel was showing the latest weather bulletin. The Boxing Day forecast had lots of black clouds spewing out rain all over the country, so nothing unusual there.

According to the presenter, there had been huge snowfalls on the Eastern US coast over Christmas. Kay vowed next year she was going to go somewhere snowy for Christmas. Perhaps she should go back to Rovaniemi but for the winter solstice this time. Then she could see the Aurora Borealis. Nothing and no one could stop her now from doing these things.

At 5pm exactly, the main national news came on. The local murders were once again the lead item. Kay watched as the channel's main news anchor, a middle-aged man in a grey suit and hair to match, delivered the latest update.

"Detectives hunting the killer of three women in Oxfordshire who were raped and stabbed during the past week have today issued a £25,000 reward for information to help catch 'The Christmas Killer', as the murderer has become known."

The picture on the screen behind the newscaster switched to the road next to the woody path, just as Kay had seen it earlier that day, with police and media everywhere.

"The latest victim, Polish national Anna Wiśniewski, died after being knifed less than 200 yards from her home late last night."

Kay looked on, horrified, as the image of Anna, the kind and downtrodden girl from the chip shop, was flashed onto the screen.

Chapter Eighteen
December 2018

Suddenly things had become very horrible and very real.

The news reported terrible events like this all the time, but they were always things happening far away and to people that she didn't know. Being local, this story had caught her attention more than most but until now, not personally knowing the victims, had still left her with a fair degree of detachment.

Now things were different. The loss of the lovely, young girl's life, who had been so kind to Kay at a time when no one else would, caused her to begin sobbing uncontrollably. How could anyone have done this to her? Anna would never have harmed a fly. It was bad enough that the poor girl had been bullied and abused by McVie while she was alive, but to lose her life in such horrific circumstances was an absolute tragedy.

The footage switched to a picture of a policewoman she recognised from the scene earlier. It was Hannah Benson, one of the local police officers. She was being interviewed by Seema Mistry at the scene.

"We're offering this reward because we must catch this evil man before he kills again," said Hannah. "Someone out there must know something. Please, if you have any information, anything at all, that you think may help our investigation, come and talk to us."

Kay switched off the television, grabbing a tissue to wipe the tears away from her eyes. She didn't have any information she could give Hannah yet, but she was going to make damned sure she soon would. The evil animal that had killed Anna was going to be brought to justice and she was the one who was going to make it happen.

She decided against ringing Kent in case his wife wanted to know who was calling and sent him a text instead, confirming that she would meet him in the pub later in the evening.

Kay was nervous walking to the pub and stuck to the well-lit main roads. Even if she didn't fit the profile of the other victims, she certainly wasn't taking any chances.

By 8pm, she was banging on the thick, wooden door of The Red Lion. The curtains were closed and the place looked deserted, but a few seconds later, the door opened a crack and she was surprised to see Andy peering around from the other side.

"It's alright!" shouted Andy back into the pub. "It's just Kent's bit of stuff."

"Let her in, then," she heard Craig call.

Andy opened up the door and said, "Sorry about that. Craig doesn't want anyone to know he's open tonight. It's strictly a private party, just for his friends."

"How come you are here, then?" quipped Kay.

"Me and Craig, we're old muckers, we are. Go back years, we do," protested Andy.

"I expect you are," remarked Kay. "You've probably paid for his pension by now."

"Any chance of a Christmas kiss, then?" he asked, gesturing at a sprig of mistletoe he had crudely attached to the top of his trousers directly above his crotch.

"You must be joking," replied Kay, thinking what a twat he was. Still, the little exchange of banter had temporarily alleviated the distress she still felt at the death of Anna.

Making her way over towards the bar, Kay could see that there was a small but select group of drinkers in the pub, about fifteen in total. They were all people she recognised, mostly long-time regulars, middle-aged divorcees and losers like Andy who had no one else to spend Christmas Day with.

It was quite a sorry-looking crowd if she was being honest. She used to wonder what had gone wrong in these people's lives for them to end up in such a state until she become one of them herself.

Kent was at the bar with Nobby, who was rabbiting on about the horses as usual. She also recognised the captain of the pub's newly formed quiz team. The others had nicknamed him 'The Beast' after a character on a teatime TV quiz show on account of his vast knowledge and opinions on all manner of trivial subjects. He had been boring her silly at the bar a few nights ago with some theory about the Star of Bethlehem being an alien spaceship.

"The worst thing about Christmas is that there's no racing for three days," said Nobby. "Thank God it's Boxing Day tomorrow and we can get back to normal: I'm getting withdrawal symptoms."

"Can't you go on the fruit machine or something?" said Kent, gesturing towards the large, noisy box with flashing lights in the corner.

"There's no value in them things," said Nobby. "Strictly for mugs, they are. Now, listen, you want to take my advice. I've been running tomorrow's cards through the computer and I'm telling you now, I've got the winner of the King George at Kempton Park. It's going to piss down tonight and this thing's been waiting for soft ground. Absolutely nailed on, it is."

"Well, good luck with that, then," said Kent, who had lost interest in betting after an attempt at a time-travelling betting coup on Auroras Encore in the 2013 Grand National had gone awry.

"I can name every King George winner since it started in 1937," boasted The Beast, who was like a walking Wikipedia on such matters. He wasn't the captain of the quiz team for nothing.

"I bet you can," said Kent, who had spotted Kay approaching the bar and needed an out from the conversation. "Why don't you tell them all to Nobby here."

The Beast turned to Nobby and started listing horses, which gave Kent an opportunity to greet Kay.

"What are you drinking?" he asked her.

"The usual," replied Kay. "Double vodka and Coke."

Kay had decided that now she was getting her life back, she was going to cut out the binge drinking. When she was at rock bottom, she had drunk to drown her sorrows, but those particular problems were behind her now.

However, tonight was an exception. The news of Anna's death had hit her hard. She needed a drink tonight. She could make staying off the booze her New Year's resolution, once all of this was over.

The two of them made their way over to their usual table and sat down, ignoring the usual jibes from Andy who was still revelling in his role as impromptu doorman. He seemed proud of his temporarily acquired status, unaware that he had only been sent over there to give the others at the bar a bit of peace from him.

"I can't believe poor Anna's dead," said Kay.

"You knew her?" asked Kent.

218

"Yes, she worked in the chip shop below my flat. She was a lovely girl, always friendly and hard-working, even though her boss exploited her and treated her like crap. I just can't believe this has happened."

Kay began to cry again. Kent reached over and took her hand, not caring whether Andy noticed or not.

"Don't let her death be in vain, Kay," said Kent. "I'm sure you've thought this over. You know what you have to do."

"Yes, I have," replied Kay, "I have to go back two days and find the killer. I can't save her, though. Whatever I do back there, she'll still be dead here."

"I know. It's too late for Anna now, but you can potentially save future victims. It's vital this monster's caught before he kills again. That's three in eight days. We need to move fast."

"Even if I do find out, will the police believe us? Would you have believed me?"

"I don't know, to be honest," replied Kent. "I've never been put in this situation. Would you believe it? All those years in the police force and I never got anywhere near a murder. As soon as I retire, three come along at once. But I've still got contacts on the force. Now would be a good time to use them."

"So what's the plan, then?" asked Kay.

"Find out who the murderer is," replied Kent. "Then, when you get back, we'll go and see Hannah together. She'll

219

have to hear me out. She owes me that much after all our years working together. Even if we don't have any evidence, we'll find a way to make her listen."

"OK, well, before I go back, I need to find out as much information as I can about the night of the murder," said Kay. "I only know what we've been told by the TV news. I know where she was killed, but do we know when?"

"Not exactly," said Kent. "I could try and find out more from Hannah, but it might look a bit odd, me making enquiries, bearing in mind it's not supposed to be anything to do with me anymore."

"So what do you suggest, then? I go and camp out in the woods all night, wait for her to come along and then watch her get butchered to death?"

"There's no need for you to freeze your tits off in the woods," replied Kent. "That lot up there at the bar were talking about this earlier and said that Anna was in here last night. So was I, but I don't recall seeing her, but then I've never met her before, so I would have been unlikely to have noticed her – it was packed again last night. Craig reckons she was hanging out with that group of teenagers that are always around the pool table."

"If that's true, then surely all I've got to do is go back to yesterday, come down here for the evening and then follow her home?" asked Kay.

"In a nutshell," replied Kent. "And I'll be here, too. I can help you."

"But you won't know about any of this then, will you?" asked Kay. "It'll be a different version of you from before the murder happened."

"You're right, I won't, but I'm sure I'll believe you if you explain it all to me. Then I will be able to help."

"I hope so," said Kay.

"Well, that's settled, then," said Kent. "You are about to become the world's first time-travelling detective. I wish I could come with you, but I've used all six of my days up."

"At least one version of you will still be involved," said Kay. "It's just you that won't remember any of it. It will be just the same as when I met your other self at the summer ball."

"All these different versions of us running about could make this quite complicated," replied Kent. "It is a shame we can't go back in time together. If only the angel had given us unlimited trips back in time. We could have set up our own time-travelling detective agency."

"Partners in time," suggested Kay.

"Brilliant," said Kent. "Perhaps we should pitch that idea to the angel. You never know."

Kay liked that idea. She would bear it in mind.

221

"I think I'm more or less ready to go, then," she said. "I will be leaving tomorrow morning, so make sure you are free afterwards. Like you say, the sooner he is behind bars, the less chance he can kill again."

"Agreed," replied Kent. "Now let's go back to the bar and see what else we can find out."

They didn't get much more information out of the regulars. Andy was back on his stool, having reached his usual level of drunken incoherence where it was not worth attempting to have a conversation with him about anything. Meanwhile, The Beast and Nobby were taking it in turns, seeing how many teams they could name that had played in the Premiership since it had started in 1992.

But Craig was a little more helpful. Apparently, the police had been in and spoken to him. He was pretty sure that Anna had left sometime after midnight and long before the pub had closed at 2am. It was a bit vague, but a useful starting point.

When Kent offered to walk Kay home, it was an offer she gratefully accepted. Deep down, she knew that she probably wouldn't be a target for the killer. All of the girls had been young and all had been of Eastern European origin. But even if she didn't fit the profile, there was still fear in her heart.

It wasn't irrational. No woman in her right mind would have wanted to walk home alone after what had happened the previous night, no matter what her age or race. It simply wasn't worth the risk.

She enjoyed being escorted home by Kent. She couldn't remember the last time a man had bothered to walk her home unless he was expecting to get some sex out of it.

At the door, she bid him goodnight with a quick peck on the cheek and decided to go straight to bed. She needed to be razor-sharp for the mission that lay ahead of her the next day.

Chapter Nineteen
December 2018

Kay was woken early by heavy raindrops lashing against the bedroom window. The gloomy weather forecast had been right.

Her thoughts were preoccupied with the day ahead. What would the angel make of what she was planning to do? As far as Kay could see, it wasn't breaking any rules, just as her quest to get her house back hadn't. Wanting to get started as quickly as possible, she got straight up and started to get dressed.

With her bathroom functions concluded and two cups of coffee inside her, she again faced her youthful reflection in the wardrobe mirror. There was no point trying to hide her intentions: she may as well just come straight out with it.

"I only want to go back two days this time," she began. "A young girl was murdered in this town on Christmas Eve and I want to find out who did it. Is that OK?"

"There's no reason why you can't do that," replied the angel, as Kay had hoped. "You are not the first to make such a request. However, you are going to need to be very careful."

"How do you mean?" asked Kay.

"Remember, as soon as you arrive back there, you are starting an alternate timeline. Everything you say and everything you do could potentially change things from that moment onwards. If you want to find out who committed this murder, you can't risk doing anything that might change the natural course of events leading up to it."

"I have already thought about that," said Kay. "I am going to speak to Richard when I get back there and work out a plan."

"That just emphasises my point," replied the angel. "Just by talking to him, you are making a change. What if he was the murderer? He might decide to kill you instead, and then where would you be?"

Kay dismissed this suggestion without a second thought.

"There's no way it could be him. I've known him most of my life and there's no way he's a murderer, not in this universe or any other."

"Are you sure about that? They do say it's the ones you least suspect," said the angel.

"Well, I'll take that risk," replied Kay. "It was partly his idea that I do this anyway, I hardly think he would have suggested it if he was the killer. As for changing things by talking to him, that doesn't worry me. He's an old hand at this time-travelling lark by now. He knows the rules and wants to find out who the murderer is just as much as I do. He won't do anything to jeopardise that."

"Well, I shall be keeping a close eye on you to see how you get on," said the angel. "Are you ready to go?"

"As ready as I'll ever be," replied Kay. "Let's get this show on the road."

Complying with her request, the angel sent her on her way. The room dissolved as she took her short temporal trip back by 48 hours."

"I thought I'd seen the last of this place," she said out loud as she once again found herself looking around her gloomy little flat. She was back where she had started two days ago, on Christmas Eve. It felt like a lot longer than that. From her perspective, it was, considering the extra days she had spent away time-travelling since then.

She remembered what the angel had said about not altering things, but what about things that had nothing to do with Anna's death? She did not see any point in going through the exact routine she had on Christmas Eve before. There was no need to go back to her old house to evict Alan and Lucy all over again. That was done and dusted in her original timeline, and there was no need to re-enact it.

Not following that path surely would not have any impact on what was going to happen to Anna. The events were completely independent of each other. Unless by some unlikely twist of fate Alan was the murderer, Kay didn't see how he could be, as he would have been safely tucked up in bed with Lucy in The Oxfordshire at the time of Anna's death.

Her thoughts turned again to the ill-fated Anna. Kay wanted so much to see the girl again one last time, but how could she look her in the eye, knowing the grisly end that awaited her? She simply couldn't face it. Every gut instinct would want to warn her or drop some hint to help her get home safely.

But that would defeat the whole object of coming back here, and for what? To give her a few more hours of life in a universe that was soon to be deleted? No, she had to keep her distance from Anna, at least until the time of the attack.

How else could she spend the day? She certainly had no intention of going to work. She hadn't gone in her original timeline, risking being sacked, so she certainly wasn't going in this universe where it didn't matter.

The best thing she could do would be to stay out of everyone's way until the evening. This meant either getting out of town or staying in the flat all day. The latter wasn't exactly her idea of fun but with barely two pennies to rub together, she could hardly go off enjoying herself.

The one thing she did need to do as soon as possible was to have a conversation with the Kent of Universe 2.0. His experience and advice would be invaluable.

Kay was trying to remember how much she had told Kent about her time-travelling at this stage. Keeping track of the days was getting very confusing and she was in danger of tying her brain up in knots with all the toing and froing through time. She needed to clarify in her mind what conversations had taken place and when.

She sat on the bed and thought it through. Today was December 24th so it must have been the previous night that she and Kent had had their tête-à-tête following her return from the day of the ball. That was fine, then: she could relax. They would have discussed enough by that stage for there to be no difficulty getting him to believe her.

She hadn't seen him on the original version of Christmas Eve, so that would need to change. She knew he had been in the pub in the evening because he had enquired about her absence, but she couldn't wait until the evening. She needed to speak to him sooner than that. Perhaps she could get his attention with a text. She pulled out her phone and began to tap on the screen.

Need to speak to you urgently. It's a matter of life and death. I've travelled back in time from Boxing Day to unmask the Christmas Killer. He's going to kill again today. Interested? Kay x x

She pressed send, wondering whether or not it had been a good idea to put the kisses on the end, but it was done now.

It was a matter of seconds before her phone rang. Kay had certainly grabbed his attention. She explained briefly what she was doing, and why, and then they arranged to meet up in town.

They met in the quietest of three branches of a chain of coffee shops that were slowly taking over the town. Kay didn't like the place at all, but it did provide a degree of anonymity, something Kent had insisted on. She preferred Josie's, but there was no way they could go there as that was where Kent's wife worked.

Fortunately, Kent offered to pay for the coffee which was just as well, as she couldn't afford the prices for their fancy drinks. They were twice the price of the coffee in Josie's. Settling down over their drinks, Kay explained the situation in more detail.

"So there you have it," she concluded. "Tonight, poor Anna's going to get raped and butchered to death on the woody path opposite the park and I intend to be there to find out who did it."

"I think it's a great idea," said Kent. "You're making far more constructive use of your days than I did."

"I thought you would approve," replied Kay. "You said it was a good idea in the other timeline, too. Back there, two days in the future, your other self is waiting for me and we are going to go to D.I. Benson together with the information."

"Yes, that's probably going to be the toughest bit," said Kent. "Hannah doesn't exactly rate me on my detecting skills. I'm not sure exactly how we are going to persuade her, but we can discuss that when you get back. In the meantime, we need to concentrate on making sure nothing goes wrong today."

"OK, so let's go over what we know," said Kay. "We know Anna was in The Red Lion until after midnight, before walking home, presumably alone. We know where she was killed, or at least where the body was found. So all we need to do is follow her and see what happens."

"That's where things start to get tricky," said Kent. "When the killer struck, he must have taken care to ensure there was no one else around. If he sees you following her up the road, it's going to put him off, isn't it?"

"Good point," replied Kay. "So how do we work around that?"

"How about if I go up to the woods and hide out there about midnight?" said Kent. "You wait in the pub, then text me when Anna leaves. That way, I'll know when to expect her, and we shouldn't spook the killer from carrying out his plan."

"This sounds so wrong," replied Kay. "It's almost as if we are aiding and abetting him."

"We're not because it's already happened and everything in this universe is going to cease to exist. I'm not feeling particularly good about that myself, to tell you the truth."

"Why?" asked Kay.

"Think about it," said Kent. "This version of me, the new one that's been created by you coming back here, well, I am effectively going to die at the end of today."

"But you'll still be alive in the other universe," replied Kay.

"That's true, I will, but it won't be the same me that is physically here right now. As soon as you arrived here this morning when the angel created this new universe, you effectively signed the death warrants of everyone in it."

"I hadn't thought of it that way before," said Kay. "But that's not going to harm any of these people, is it? None of them know that it's not the real universe. When the angel deletes it, they will just disappear. It's not like they will die a painful death, screaming in agony, is it?"

"But I know," replied Kent glumly. "Whatever I do today, this version of me is now effectively doomed."

"Look at it positively," said Kay. "You are free from consequences just as much as I am now. You can do whatever you want."

She thought about suggesting they rekindle their romance but stopped short. Although that would be a fun way to spend the afternoon, it was the sort of thing the old Kay would have done and she was turning over a new leaf now.

"I could do whatever I wanted, but I've already been there and bought the T-shirt. What I really ought to do is focus on helping you unmask this killer," replied Kent. "What do you think of my plan to wait in the woods?"

"In principle, it's great," replied Kay. "But I can see a flaw in that plan."

"What's that?" asked Kent.

"If you are up there unmasking the killer and I'm still in the pub, I won't know who did it, will I?" reasoned Kay.

"Well, I'll tell you afterwards," said Kent.

"What if it's not that easy?" asked Kay. "What if he spots you and you get into a fight? He might even kill you! Or what if I get whisked back to Boxing Day before you have time to tell me? It's putting too much uncertainty into the mix. I think your plan is good, but we need to swap places. I need to be in the woods and you need to be in the pub."

"You could just as easily get killed yourself," said Kent. "Have you thought about that?"

"Would that matter?" said Kay. "None of this is real so I'll just end up alive again on Boxing Day."

"Are you sure about that?" asked Kent. "Your body here might not be your own, but what about your soul? If you die here, in this body, could the very essence of you not die with it?"

"I hadn't thought of that," said Kay, feeling a tad uncomfortable. "Otherwise I would have asked the angel before I left. I guess I'll just have to be extra careful and make sure it doesn't happen."

"OK, good. It looks like we've got ourselves the making of a plan, then," said Kent. "And now I am going to have to go. Debs wants me to pick up our turkey from the butcher's and they are closing at lunchtime today. If I don't come back with it, she'll skin me alive and roast me instead, I expect. And I've no desire to experience that in this universe, or any other."

"We shall meet in the pub later, then," said Kay, still wondering what she was going to do for the rest of the day. She needed some money if she was going to enjoy it. Would it be rude to ask him? She couldn't see why not, under the circumstances.

"Just one thing, before you go," she added. "Could you lend me a few quid? Well, more than a few, really. A couple of hundred would be nice. After all, it's not like you're going to need it after today, is it?"

"I suppose not," said Kent gloomily, still reflecting on the mortality of his current body.

"I'm skint at the moment and since I've used up one of my days coming back here for a good cause it would be nice if I could enjoy a bit of it," she added.

"What are you going to spend all that on?" asked Kent.

"Oh, just a bit of pampering," said Kay, remembering her impromptu trip to London on her earlier trip. "I don't want to be stuck up in that horrible flat all day, not with the landlord threatening to cut my electricity off. And he is definitely going to do that, today, because he did it before. I'll book myself into the Travelodge."

It would be a far cry from her previous jaunt to the hotel in Mayfair but she couldn't go too far, not with the evening that lay ahead. All she really wanted was a hot bath, some decent food and some warmth. Most importantly of all, she didn't want to see that accursed flat again, or risk encountering McVie.

"Fair enough," said Kent. "I blew a fair amount of cash on some of my trips back in time. We'll stop off at the cashpoint on the way to the butcher's."

Parting company with Kent, a generous £200 in her handbag, she made first for New Look to get some clean clothes. Next, she stopped at Wilko's for some toiletries, before taking a taxi to the Travelodge where she spent a long, lazy afternoon in warmth and comfort, watching crappy Christmas movies on the TV and taking full advantage of room service.

By the time the early evening rolled around, she was fit and ready for action.

Chapter Twenty
December 2018

Kay had arranged to meet Kent in the pub at 10pm. That was much later than she usually went out but she didn't want to get sucked into a long-drawn-out drinking session. This was difficult to avoid in The Red Lion at the best of times, but even more so on Christmas Eve when the booze would be flowing freely.

Kent was already there when she arrived, standing at the bar with Andy and the others. She went straight over to join him, and ordered a drink, sticking to just a single vodka with a lot of Coke. She felt incredibly nervous knowing what was to come and could quite easily have knocked back a neat double, but was determined to keep a clear head. She needed to be professional about what she was doing tonight.

As soon as Kent saw her, he moved away from the bar, gesturing at her to move further up the pub away from the other regulars.

"Sorry about that," he said, joining her at the bar, out of view of the others in the crowded bar. "But I didn't want you to have to put up with any of Andy's crap. He saw me giving you that money at the cashpoint earlier and is telling everyone I'm paying you for sex now."

"What a cheek," remarked Kay. "I really could slap that twat at times."

"Well, there's no point doing anything about it," said Kent. "It's all irrelevant in this universe. As is Nobby and The Beast's argument about what is the best Christmas Number One of all time, which has been going on for well over half an hour."

"I'm glad I missed that," said Kay.

"Now then, about Anna," said Kent.

"Have you seen her?" asked Kay.

"Yes, she's over there at the pool table," replied Kent.

Kay looked over and spotted Anna straightaway. She was playing pool with Lauren and her usual group of young male followers. She was struck by how pretty Anna looked. Kay had only ever seen her in her chip shop overalls with her hair tied back in a bun.

Tonight she looked stunning, the curves of her full figure perfectly complemented by the long, black dress she was wearing. Her blonde hair, straight and smooth, flowed down beneath her shoulders now it was no longer tied up. Resisting the temptation to go over and speak to her, Kay turned back to Kent.

"Have you spotted anything unusual? Have any weirdos been hanging around or anything like that? What about those lads who are always sniffing around Lauren? Could it be one of them?"

"No, nothing out of the ordinary at all," replied Kent. "She's been over there with the underage drinkers for the past hour. I can't see it being one of them: they're just harmless kids as far as I can see."

"I think it's best that we stay over here at a safe distance, then," suggested Kay, bearing in mind their earlier conversation. "We need to avoid interaction, if at all possible."

The pool table was less than ten yards away from where they were standing but it was quite easy to blend into the background. The pub was heaving with people and very noisy with the disco blaring out. It was so crowded that Kay even managed to visit the ladies, the door to which was right behind the pool table, without Anna spotting her.

So far, so good, but she couldn't avoid being spotted indefinitely. The youths at the pool table were knocking back the booze like it was going out of fashion, frequently visiting the bar to stock up on drinks and shots. Shortly after Kay had returned to the bar, it was Anna's turn to get a round in.

With Kent having nipped off to the gents, there was a space at the bar right next to Kay and Anna made a beeline straight for it.

Kay tried to turn away to hide her face but it was too late. Anna had already spotted her and bounced over, full of festive cheer.

"Kay! Merry Christmas," she said, in her Polish accent. "Is everything OK with you? I heard Mr McVie say he was going to turn off your electricity at lunchtime."

She was showing genuine concern, which was so like her. Desperately trying to hide the unbearable emotions churning away inside her, Kay just about managed to reply without her voice cracking.

"It's OK, Anna, I haven't been home. I'm staying away for Christmas, so McVie can do whatever he likes."

"I think he is very cruel to you," said Anna. "I hope maybe you can find somewhere else to live soon?"

"I hope so," replied Kay. "And maybe you should find somewhere else to work. You really should not let him abuse you like he does. The things he was saying the other day were nothing short of bullying, not to mention racist."

Kay knew these words were pointless, knowing that the girl would never see another dawn, let alone find another job. She just wanted to let her know that not everyone in the town thought the way McVie did. It was a tiny crumb of comfort, not a lot to take with her to the grave, but what else did Kay have to offer?

"It's not easy," replied Anna. "Although my family has been here seven years, it is hard to find jobs that pay well. The bosses think we will work for very little because we are from Poland, but it is very expensive to live here."

While Anna was speaking, Kay glanced up and was horrified to see the bloated figure of McVie approaching behind her. This was all she needed. What was he doing in here? She had never seen him in the pub before. He must be one of those once-a-year drinkers that just came out at Christmas.

"Well, well, well, if it isn't Lil' Miss Gummy," remarked McVie. "I want a word with you."

"Whatever you've got to say, I'm not interested," said Kay, and she meant it. He had no hold over her anymore, in this universe or the other one, so for once she could speak her mind.

"I told you I wanted that rent by today. And where were you when I came up to collect it? In here, I suppose, like the drunken old slag you are. No wonder you can't afford to pay my rent if you're pissing all your money up in the pub. So don't bother trying to put the lights on when you get home: they won't work."

"Do you think I give a fuck?" retorted Kay. "You can shove your shitty little flat up your arse."

"Careful, missy," said McVie, leering towards her. "You don't want to get on the wrong side of me." He made no attempt to disguise the threat in his voice.

He hadn't noticed Anna yet, as she had been standing with her back to him the whole time, but now the young Polish girl turned around and let fly with both barrels.

239

"Why don't you leave her alone?" she yelled, taking both him and Kay by surprise. "I think you are a very cruel and horrible man, Mr McVie."

"Oh, so you're here as well, are you? So that's why you wanted the night off," said McVie. "And there was me thinking you were going to have a nice cosy evening with however many brothers and sisters you brought over here with you. Clearly, I've been paying you too much if you can afford to come drinking in this place."

"You pay me five pounds per hour and it's exploitation," responded Anna.

"Yeah, well, that's probably a fortune in your country. You should be glad there are people like me who are willing to let you come over here and work. In your case, however, you don't work for me anymore. As of this moment, you can consider yourself sacked."

"You can't do that," said Kay. "Anna was just sticking up for me. Take it out on me if you are going to take it out on anyone."

She looked towards the gents, willing Kent to get a move on as she could desperately use some backup, but there was no sign of him.

"I think you'll find I can do whatever I want," replied McVie. "She's got no contract, no paperwork, in fact, nothing at all to prove she ever worked for me. Do you think I want all that paperwork and expense – tax and National Insurance?

240

Bollocks to that. Foreigners work cash in hand, no questions asked. They like it that way, and so do I."

Turning back to Anna, he added, "And that means I don't even need to pay you this week's wages. Merry Christmas." He started laughing.

"I want what you owe me," said Anna. Kay could see she was fighting back the tears, as she tried to stick up to this vile man. "I am going to tell my brothers about this."

"What, that bunch of unemployed illegal immigrants?" asked McVie. "Do you think I'm scared of them?"

"What's going on here?" asked Kent, who had finally emerged from the toilets and caught the tail-end of the conversation.

"This man is making a nuisance of himself," said Kay.

"Is he now?" asked Kent. "Look here, mate, I suggest you move along and stop bothering these ladies."

"Why, what are you going to do, arrest me?" replied McVie. "Oh no, you can't do that anymore, can you? Not that you ever could. I know who you are, pal. You're that crap policeman who can't catch any criminals. The one that got kicked out and replaced by a woman! You're a fucking laughing stock, mate."

Even though the pub was packed and the disco was blaring out, the argument was beginning to attract attention. Thankfully help had now arrived from behind the bar. One of the barmaids, sensing trouble, had called Craig over and he now intervened.

"He may not be able to arrest you, but this is my pub and I say who does or doesn't drink here. Any more crap out of you, and you're out. Now shift yourself elsewhere, away from these people, or you're out."

McVie reluctantly complied, but he threw a filthy look at Kay and Anna as he moved away, letting them know in no uncertain terms that this wasn't over.

"What am I going to do now?" asked Anna. "I needed that job."

"Don't worry," replied Kay. "You can't do anything now until after Christmas. Just try and enjoy the night."

What else could she say?

Anna's friend, Lauren, had come over to the bar now. She had been far enough away by the pool table not to hear what was going on. That was probably just as well, thought Kay. She had seen how feisty Lauren could get, and if she had been drawn into the argument as well, all hell could have broken loose.

"What's taking so long with these drinks?" asked Lauren, swaying about, clearly drunk.

"Just coming now," said Anna, putting a brave face on things. "Here, give me a hand." She passed a couple of bottles of lager to Lauren and picked up a tray containing the rest of the drinks. Just before she left, she turned back to Kay.

"Thank you for sticking up for me, Kay," she said.

"I thought it was the other way round," replied Kay.

"We stuck for each other. You are a good friend, I think," replied Anna, smiling. She took the tray and made her way carefully through the crowded bar towards the pool table.

That smile well and truly broke Kay's heart. She knew they were probably the last words Anna would ever speak to her.

With Anna safely out of earshot, Kent said, "Was that a good idea? You're not meant to be getting involved with her. What happened back there could have changed things irretrievably. What if she decides to go home early because of it?"

"I didn't have a lot of choice," replied Kay. "She spotted me when she came to the bar: I could hardly blank her. Why were you so long in the toilet, anyway? If you'd not left me for so long, a lot of that could have been avoided."

"Yeah, I'm sorry about that," replied Kent. "I was on the toilet. Deb's sister called around with some of her homemade mince pies earlier. I don't know what she puts in them. They taste gorgeous, but they always go straight through me."

"Too much information," stated Kay. She found the idea of taking a dump in a pub toilet repulsive and certainly didn't want to hear about it.

"Sorry," said Kent. "Let's have one more drink, and then you had better be thinking about getting yourself in position."

The disco seemed to be getting louder and was now belting out a selection of Christmas classics. When "I Wish It Could Be Christmas Everyday" came on, Kay reflected that, just recently, it really had been for her.

They lost sight of Anna for a while as she headed over to the dance floor with Lauren and their group of friends. The pub was full of young people tonight. Kay was relieved to see that Maddie was not among them.

A potential complication she had feared was that her daughter might turn up here tonight. Such a meeting could have been a distraction, not to mention awkward. In this timeline, there had been no reconciliation between them. But thankfully Maddie was not here. It was highly likely that she was in The Wheatsheaf, a goths' and rockers' pub up the other end of town which was more her scene.

McVie's continued presence was also a worry, but they didn't have any more trouble with him. They could see his flabby frame leaning against a wooden beam at the edge of the dance floor, downing pints of lager with a face like thunder. He didn't seem to be speaking to anyone very much, but that didn't surprise Kay. The way he went on, she didn't expect that he had many friends.

At half past eleven she took her leave of Kent to head to the woods, heeding his many warnings to take care. Meanwhile, he took up a new position further along the bar where he could better observe the dance floor area.

It was very cold outside again and getting foggy, but Kay was prepared, having bought herself a nice, thick Christmas jumper during the afternoon. It wasn't as cold in the woods, where the trees offered a degree of protection from the freezing wind. For the next half an hour she kept in touch with Kent via text, as he provided her with regular updates.

Just after midnight, he texted to say that Anna's friend, Lauren, had gone. Apparently, she had left with some bloke, her tongue practically halfway down his throat. That might explain why Anna had ended up going home alone.

A few minutes later her phone vibrated to let her know she had a call. Concealed behind a tree, she had put her phone on silent, just in case the killer was already around. The last thing she wanted was her mobile ringing out, alerting anyone to her presence.

"She's just left and she's walking up the High Street," Kent informed her. "She should be with you in about ten minutes."

"OK, well, I had better ring off now," said Kay, as quietly as she could. "I can't risk being detected."

"I'm going to give it another five minutes and then start heading slowly your way," replied Kent. "Ring me and let me know when it's all over and I'll come straight to you. I think you're being incredibly brave, by the way. Good luck."

"Thank you," said Kay, and hung up. She didn't feel incredibly brave. She felt terrified. This was a terrifying situation to be in, alone in the freezing woods, about to be witness to a grisly murder. It was dark, too, there being no lighting on the woody path.

Right on schedule, ten minutes later, she peered around the tree and just about picked out the solitary figure of Anna walking towards her out of the thickening fog. She checked her watch. It was 12.32am. She made a note of the time: it might come in useful later.

Kay shrank back undercover and listened, as the girl approached. Then she heard a male voice call out.

"Anna," he called.

It was a voice Kay recognised immediately and a dreadful realisation dawned. Of course, it all made sense now.

"What do you want?" replied Anna. "Leave me alone."

"I wanted to apologise for earlier," came the reply. "I didn't mean what I said. You can have your job back. I'll even give you the minimum wage if that helps."

Kay could not resist another quick peek around the tree, even though the two of them were only about twenty yards away. She didn't even need visual confirmation of his rotund frame to know that it was McVie who was speaking.

Kay felt a feeling of impending doom as she realised what the true reason was behind this uncharacteristic show of reconciliation. The trusting, young girl was about to fall right into his clutches.

"Really?" said Anna.

The Polish girl stopped and turned back to face him, allowing him to walk right up to her. It was a fatal mistake, one for which she was about to pay with her life.

"Of course not, you stupid cow," said McVie, pulling out a knife and grabbing hold of her. Anna screamed, but he swiftly cut her off with a hand over her mouth.

"Have a go at me in the pub, would you? Make me look stupid? You don't even belong in this country. Now keep still, bitch, unless you want me to slit your throat."

Anna wriggled in an attempt to break free. She was way younger and fitter than the sweating, mound of blubber who was trying to force himself upon her, but what he lacked in fitness he had in weight. Forcing her to the ground, he put the full weight of his twenty stone on top of her, pinning her down and making her gasp for air. It was the same move he had tried to do to Kay in her flat a few days before.

She simply couldn't bear to watch any more of this. Whatever may be set in stone in her timeline, this was happening here and now and there was no way she could stand idly by and let this version of the terrified girl be raped and murdered in front of her.

She knew the identity of the attacker now. That was what she had come here to find out. So was there any need for this temporary version of Anna to suffer? There wasn't and Kay simply had to do something.

With McVie now tearing at the girl's clothes, Kay launched herself out from behind the tree and ran right at him in an attempt to push him away. He was much heavier than she was, but she carried enough speed for her mighty shove to knock him off her. As he struggled to regain his balance, temporarily confused by the surprise attack, Anna managed to scramble free.

"Run, Anna!" shouted Kay. "Just run and don't look back!"

"Oh, you've done it now!" shouted McVie, a crazed look in his eyes as he recovered sufficiently to grab hold of Kay, knife in hand. "You are so fucking dead."

"Kay," screamed Anna, seemingly rooted to the spot.

"Go and get help!" shouted Kay. Relieved, she saw Anna turn and begin to run.

"You're dead," hissed McVie.

Terrified as she was, Kay felt a strange sense of detachment as she saw the knife flash before her. He was holding her down with one hand and wielding the knife with

248

the other, as he brought it down against her neck. At first, the steel felt cold against her skin, then strangely warm. With a sickening shock, she realised he had slit her throat and felt consciousness begin to slip away from her.

"Please don't let this be the end" was her final thought as she drifted away, desperately hoping that the angel would be watching over her, ready to whisk her home.

Chapter Twenty-One
December 2018

Suddenly Kay was back in front of the wardrobe mirror in her bedroom. She may have been back in her original body, but the sensations from the experience she had just been through still coursed through her. Like waking from a nightmare, she felt a sense of panic as conflicting signals in her brain sent her into a state of shock, believing that her throat in this body had been slit, too.

Unable to see her true reflection with the image of the angel looking back at her, instinctively her hand went to her neck to check that her skin remained unbroken. The relief she felt in discovering herself intact did nothing to alleviate her feelings. Shaking with fear and adrenalin, she turned and flopped onto the bed, sobbing her heart out at the horrific ordeal she had just endured.

After a minute or two, she composed herself and sat up on the bed, looking into the mirror. The angel was still there but hadn't spoken during Kay's traumatic last few moments. Now, as Kay wiped the tears from her eyes, the angel spoke.

"Better now?" she asked.

"I'm not sure I'll ever be better again," replied Kay. "I've just discovered what it feels like to die."

"It's just as well I got you out of there when I did, then," replied the angel. "In another moment or two, you would have been lost."

"Even though it wasn't the same body?" asked Kay.

"Yes," replied the angel. "It may have been a duplicate body, but the essence of what makes you, your spirit if you like, was locked up inside that body."

"You should have warned me," said Kay.

"I did try to, remember? But you were a woman on a mission."

Kay had to concede that the angel was right. She wouldn't have been able to talk Kay out of going, whatever she had said.

"Well, it's all over now," said Kay. "And I've got a killer to bring to justice."

"It seems that you do," said the angel. "So, I guess I will be seeing you tomorrow for your last trip?"

Kay hadn't even begun to think about where to go next.

"You know, after what I've just been through, I am not sure I want to go back again just yet," said Kay. "Can you give me a few more days to think about it?"

"It doesn't work like that," replied the angel. "Six days, all in a row, that's the deal. You can't bank them for future use."

"Yes, but imagine the good I could do if I did," argued Kay. "You saw what I achieved by going back to Christmas Eve. If I go somewhere tomorrow, it will only be for fun. I've no more mysteries to solve, wrongs to right, or anything else constructive to do in the past."

"There's nothing wrong with that, is there? Just indulge yourself. You enjoyed going to see the midnight sun, didn't you? And going back to Christmas Day as a kid?"

"Of course," said Kay. "But now I've seen the power that this gift can deliver, I feel it would be self-indulgent to waste it."

"I think you've done more than enough," said the angel. "You've been quite possibly the best subject I've ever had. You haven't just thought about yourself, and I like that. As a reward, I think you deserve to pamper yourself on this last day. Choose a special day, and just go back and enjoy it."

"If you put it like that, perhaps I should," agreed Kay. "I am sure I will think of something by tomorrow. And what happens after that? Do I never see you again?"

"That's usually how it works," replied the angel.

"That's a pity," said Kay. "Because Kent and I were talking, and we thinking how great it would be to set up a time-travelling detective agency – one where we could use our trips back in time to solve crimes and right injustices. It wouldn't be for personal gain, you understand, just two people trying to make the world a better place. I think it would be good for him,

252

too. It would finally give him the chance to solve some crimes to make amends for his less than illustrious policing career."

"I like the idea," said the angel. "And I can see the merit in what you are saying. But he's already used up his six days and you've only got one left."

"But you still think it's a good idea?"

"I said so, didn't I?" replied the angel.

"Well, then, how about allocating us some more days in the future so we can do it? Maybe give us some sort of hotline so we can call you up when we need you?"

"I'm not here at everyone's beck and call, you know," protested the angel. "There are other people I need to help. You and Kent have got your lives sorted now. I can't be running back to you every five minutes."

"That shouldn't be a problem for you if you are as omnipresent as you claim. I seem to recall you saying you could be any place at any time, so it's hardly like you need a time-management course, is it?"

"Well, I might have exaggerated a little on that front," said the angel. "But I will think about it. Meanwhile, I suggest you think about where you want to go tomorrow. I will see you then."

"Fair enough," replied Kay. "Now I must go and get on. Things to do, people to see: you know how it is."

Ten minutes later she was sitting at the kitchen table, a cup of coffee in hand and a mince pie on a plate in front of her, nice and warm after precisely seventeen seconds in the microwave. She always found getting the timing on mince pies tricky. They were either lukewarm or exploded in the microwave, but for once she had got it right.

She was feeling much calmer now, the shock of her recent experience slowly fading. Even so, she knew that the memories of the traumatic events would likely be with her for life. It wasn't the sort of thing anyone was ever likely to forget.

It was time to get to work. She reached for her mobile, and once again texted Kent.

I know who the killer is. Meet me in the pub at 12.30.

He quickly replied with his confirmation.

When she got to the pub, Kent was at the bar with Nobby, who was arguing with Craig.

"Come on, mate: put the racing on the telly. It's the King George at Kempton Park, today. I've been looking forward to this all week."

"Well, go to the bookies and watch it then," replied Craig. "Man City v Liverpool kicks off at 12.45, and that lot over there have come in to watch it."

He gestured towards a bunch of middle-aged men in Liverpool shirts.

"They've been cooped up with their families for two days, no doubt itching to get down here to watch the game. I'm not switching it off for some horse race."

"Suit yourself," said Nobby. "I was going to give you a tip I've had off a mate for a horse running at Wetherby later, but you can stick it now."

Getting up from his stool, Nobby tucked his *Racing Post* under his arm and headed for the door, muttering as he did so.

That left the bar area nice and clear for her to talk to Kent while Craig went off to serve the Liverpool supporters. She explained in detail what had happened, including the details of her own 'death' at the hands of McVie.

"So there you have it," she concluded. "We know without a doubt it was him, so what now?"

"We go to Hannah, and try and get her to bring him in," replied Kent.

"Yes, and we need to be quick about it," said Kay. "He said he was going up to Scotland for Hogmanay after Christmas. They need to catch him before he leaves."

"The big issue we have here remains evidence," said Kent. "We don't have any."

"But there's nothing to stop them taking him in for enquiries, is there? He was her boss, after all. Then they just need to take his DNA. Surely they can match it to the victims?

255

He raped them all for a start, so that will have left some evidence."

Saying these words, she winced at the sheer gruesomeness of what the nature of that evidence would be.

"Absolutely," said Kent. "But she's still got to have a reason to bring him in. There are all sorts of rules you have to follow, and I should know. I got into all sorts of trouble over not sticking to procedures over the years. It's bloody frustrating, I can tell you."

Kay nodded her understanding, as Kent continued.

"The problem with high-profile cases like this is that they attract people with crackpot theories about who could have done it, especially if there's a reward at stake. You'd be amazed how many would-be amateur sleuths there are out there. Then you've got all the vindictive types involved in petty feuds with neighbours, trying to accuse them of all sorts of things they haven't done."

"Isn't that called wasting police time?" asked Kay.

"Yes, but it doesn't stop them from doing it," said Kent. "In a case like this, Hannah's bound to have had a few down the station trying it on."

"Ah, but I've got a secret weapon, haven't I?" asked Kay.

"What's that, then?" asked Kent.

"It's you, of course. You used to be D.I. here and her old boss. She has to listen to you."

"I'm not sure that's going to cut much mustard," replied Kent. "She was dubious enough over my policing skills when I was her boss, let alone now. Still, we can but try."

"At least you can get me a foot in the door," said Kay. "Then we will just have to make her listen. Come on: let's not waste any more time. Give her a call and arrange a meeting."

An hour later, the two of them were sitting in Kent's old office at the station, now with the nameplate D.I. Benson on the door. As well as Hannah, PC Adrian Johnson, another of Kent's old team, was there.

"Well, I didn't think I'd see this old place again," said Kent, reminiscing. "I'm glad to see you haven't changed too much in here."

"No, not much," said Hannah. "Though if you were to open that filing cabinet over there you would find it now has actual files in it, as opposed to your stash of crisps and chocolates. Oh, and you left half a bottle of Scotch in there as well, by the way. I think it's still here somewhere."

"I think that was what we had on Christmas Eve," remarked Johnson. "We didn't think you'd mind. Hannah has banned drinking on duty since you left, but we had a toast to you for old times' sake after we went off duty."

"That was nice of you," remarked Kent, feeling genuinely touched. "And there was I thinking neither of you

257

liked me. You never wanted to come down the pub with me after work."

"Of course we liked you," said Hannah. "You were a real character."

"Salt of the Earth," said Adrian. "They just don't make coppers like you anymore."

Kent wasn't sure if Adrian was taking the piss or not, but decided to be gracious.

"Thank you, both of you," he said. "That means a lot."

"Now then, down to business," said Hannah. "It's very nice of you to come and visit us like this, but you did say on the phone this wasn't just a social call and you had some vital information for us."

"Well, it's Kay who's got the information, not me. I'll let her explain."

Kay briefly outlined what had happened on her version of Christmas Eve, going into great detail about exactly where and when McVie had attacked Anna. Hannah listened intently until she had finished, and now had some questions to ask.

"You say you witnessed all this. If that was the case, why have you left it until now, two days later, to come in and tell us?"

"I was terrified – traumatised, even," said Kay. "I had a lot to drink that night and carried on drinking after I got home. Then I passed out and lost track of time."

"You say you had a lot to drink. Is it not possible you imagined all this in a drunken stupor?" asked Hannah. "You also said that this man, McVie, is your landlord and he's been giving you a hard time. Next thing you accuse him of being a murderer. How am I to know you haven't just dreamt all this up as a way of getting back at him?"

"Richard said you would say that," said Kay.

"I did," said Kent. "But Hannah, listen to her, I'll vouch for her."

"Please don't take this personally, Richard, but with your track record for jumping to the wrong conclusions, I'm not about to take your endorsement as gospel. Remember that lad, Charlie, you had in here a few months back? You reckoned he was a murderer, too, and look how that turned out."

"So what are you going to do, then?" asked Kent.

"We'll look into the background of Mr McVie and talk to him, as one of several leads we are following up. I can't promise any more than that for the moment."

"That's not good enough!" exclaimed Kay. "He's killed three times in just over a week. While you are following up your leads, he could be lining up victim number four!"

"I appreciate that, but you haven't given us anything concrete to go on," replied Hannah.

"Why don't we just tell her the truth about how I really found out," said Kay, more out of desperation than hope.

"She'd never believe you," said Kent. "Who would?"

"And what is the truth?" asked Hannah.

"Don't tell her, Kay," said Kent. "You'll be laughed out of the station."

As far as Kay was concerned she had nothing to lose. She would make this stuck-up young policewoman believe her, and if she didn't she would go and sort McVie out herself.

"What would you say if I told you I had a certain advantage in terms of time?" said Kay.

"What do you mean by that?" said PC Johnson, deciding it was about time he got involved in the discussion.

"What if I told you that I had a way of travelling back in time and I had used it to find out who the killer was?" asked Kay.

Johnson erupted into peals of laughter. "Oh, my, I've heard it all now! Time travel!" Turning to Kent, incredulously, he added, "And you believe this? No wonder they drummed you out of the force."

260

Before Kent could reply, Hannah interceded. She had not shared Johnson's mirth, instead maintaining a serious and professional look on her face.

"Adrian, I'll handle this from here. Why don't you go and make us all some coffee?"

Johnson left the room, still chuckling.

"Unbelievable!" they heard him say, as the door closed behind him.

"Right, now he's gone I want to hear what you've got to say," said Hannah. "If you really have travelled in time, I want to know how."

"You're not dismissing this out of hand, then?" asked Kent, scarcely able to believe that the level-headed Hannah was even entertaining the notion.

"Let's just say I've got an open mind about this sort of thing," said Hannah. "But before we go any further, let's get one thing clear. Whatever is said between the three of us in this room from now on goes no further. We are strictly off the record."

"Agreed," said Kay and Kent in unison, both pleasantly surprised and intrigued by Hannah's interest. Kent couldn't believe for a moment that she was taking this seriously, but even if she did dismiss what Kay said, they would be no worse off than before.

Kay explained how she had travelled back in time to solve the crime, not leaving out any details. She was aware she was going against the angel's instructions not to tell anyone else, but it couldn't be helped.

"So, do you believe me now?" asked Kay.

Before Hannah could answer, Johnson returned with a tray of coffees.

"Thank you, Adrian, that'll be all," said Hannah. "Go and help out at the front desk for me, would you?"

"Whatever you say, boss. I'll give you a call if I hear of any time-travelling police boxes turning up."

Disappointed when he got no reaction to his joke, Adrian left them to it.

With him out of the way, Hannah said, "OK, I'm willing to trust what you've told me is true. I'm taking a big gamble with this, but we'll bring McVie in for questioning and I'll make sure we DNA test him, no matter how much he bleats about it. I could well end up with egg on my face over this, but I'll take this risk this once."

"Why?" asked Kent. "As soon as time travel was mentioned, I saw your interest perk up. Why didn't you react like Johnson did? The vast majority of people would have."

"Let's just say I have had some experience with this sort of thing," said Hannah.

"The angel's visited you, too?" asked Kent. "Blimey, he gets around a bit, doesn't he?"

"Not exactly," said Hannah. "I've never heard of this angel before today. My experience is more to do with going forward in time, rather than backwards."

"Well, this is an unexpected development," said Kent. "Mind you, the angel did tell me once when we were talking about time travel in this town, that there was a lot of it about."

"It only happened to me once," said Hannah. "But I know of others it has happened to as well, but I would prefer not to go into details about that. In my case, Richard, you were indirectly involved the night I time-travelled. You might even remember it."

"When was it?" asked Kent.

"It was only a couple of months ago," replied Hannah. "It was just before that unfortunate business with the missing girl. Do you remember that a couple of nights before I went missing?"

Kent racked his brains, trying to remember, but couldn't recall anything.

"You'll have to give me more than that," he said.

"OK," said Hannah, hoping to jog his memory. "Do you remember that night when you sent me and Adrian down to the railway line to investigate some yobs spraying graffiti around? Adrian had to come back to the station alone because he couldn't find me after I went to look for the kids who were doing it."

Kent remembered now. "Yes, I do. I was late getting down the pub that night because we were trying to find out where you had gone."

"Well, you'll probably also remember that when I got back here we had an argument about what time it was. That's because it was much later not only than I thought, but than what my watch was telling me. Something happened to me down at the railway line and I was transported forward about three-quarters of an hour in time."

"I gave you a right bollocking over that, didn't I?" asked Kent.

"You did. But it doesn't matter now."

"Why didn't you tell me the truth at the time?" asked Kent.

"At the time I didn't know what the truth was," replied Hannah. "I was as confused as you were. But if I had known, would you have believed me?"

"To be fair, probably not," said Kent. "I would probably have reacted like Adrian did just now. But a lot's happened since then."

"Right, well now that we've established that we all believe in time travel, let's move on," said Hannah. "I've got a killer to catch."

"Lucky you," said Kent. "I waited all those years for one to come along, then you get one in your first month on the job."

"It's hardly lucky is it?" said Hannah. "Three girls have died, remember?"

"He didn't mean it like that," said Kay.

"I know he didn't," said Hannah. "You always did speak without thinking first, Richard.

"Putting my size nines in it, Debs says," replied Kent.

"As for you Kay, I want to thank you," continued Hannah. "Were you aware that there is a reward for information leading to the killer's arrest? I will see to it personally that if this all holds up, you will get it."

Kay wasn't sure how she felt about that. It felt a bit like taking blood money, profiting from Anna's death in such a way, but she couldn't deny the money would come in handy. During her long talk with Maddie on Christmas Eve, her daughter told her how much debt she had already run up in her first term at university. The reward money would go some way to helping her out, as well as funding some plans Kay had of her own.

"Thank you," she replied. "Now go and nail that fucker."

"We will," replied Hannah.

She was true to her word. As Kay watched the evening news on the BBC, with Maddie by her side, the news of McVie's arrest was breaking.

As Maddie flicked through the special double edition of *Radio Times*, Kay relaxed with a feeling of a job well done. For the rest of the evening, they watched Christmas movies, shared a bottle of Baileys, and scoffed their way through a whole tin of Celebrations.

Kay still hadn't decided where she was going on her final trip the next day, but she didn't care anymore. She was just happy to be safely back at home with Maddie, secure in the knowledge that McVie was behind bars.

Chapter Twenty-Two
February 2019

Kay and Maddie lay side by side on sunbeds next to the swimming pool. It was February half-term and Kay had whisked Maddie away from Durham University for a much-needed week of winter sun at a hotel in Tenerife.

Kay loved going on holiday at this time of the year. Summer holidays were all well and good, but nothing could beat a good strong dose of warmth and vitamin D during a long English winter. Maddie was lapping it up, too, unlike the goths of Kay's generation who had generally stayed out of the sun.

As Maddie streamed music from Spotify and read her Kindle, Kay thought about just how much her life had changed of late. It had been just seven weeks since Christmas and she certainly hadn't been idle.

The day after Boxing Day she had seen the angel for the final time. She had decided to take the angel's advice, forget the serious stuff, and go back and enjoy a special day from her past.

Accordingly, she found herself arriving back on the date she had chosen, March 4th 1993. She had chosen to go back to the date of her first gig, that amazing night she had enjoyed at the Equinox Club in Leicester Square seeing Saint Etienne.

The night was every bit as good as she remembered, and she made sure she soaked up every second of it. It wasn't just the concert that was amazing, but also spending time with Angie and Becky, the two friends who had gone to the gig with her.

On her return, she again asked the angel about future crime-solving time travel opportunities. Reluctantly agreeing to consider it, the angel gave her a password to summon her one more time in case of an emergency, stressing not to waste it on anything trivial. She also declared that she would have a right to veto anything Kay might be asking to do.

Kay was more than happy with that and had not even considered calling the angel since. She was keeping that offer firmly under lock and key until it was absolutely needed.

McVie was charged and on the advice of his solicitor decided to plead guilty. It was pointless doing anything else. The forensic evidence the police made his conviction 100% certain. He had no defence whatsoever and in January was jailed for life.

Subsequently, Kay received the £25,000 reward money. At first, she felt wrong taking it, considering that Anna had had to lose her life for her to receive it. But Kent convinced her she was entitled to it after all she had been through, taking McVie's knife in place of Anna in Universe 2.0. And Anna would have died anyway, so it was hardly blood money.

The first thing she did when the money came through was to get her teeth fixed up. That wasn't cheap – with eight teeth missing, it ran to thousands but it was worth it.

She joined a gym, left the booze and fags behind for good, and started eating healthily. The change in her appearance in just a few short weeks was astounding.

She signed up for an Open University course in journalism, keen to revive her earlier travel and writing plans.

She also decided to keep her job at the shop for the time being, keen to save as much money as possible which wasn't difficult now she was rent- and mortgage-free. Now she had her new teeth she was even allowed back on the tills again.

Alan agreed to a quickie divorce – he didn't have much choice – and that was progressing nicely. She expected to have her decree absolute by the end of February.

As for Kent, his life was moving forward, too. Craig announced in the New Year that he was planning to sell the lease on the pub. Shortly afterwards, Kent announced that he and Debs were going to buy it and run it as a combined pub and restaurant.

With a full smile and confidence restored, Kay plucked up the courage to seek out Robert, the man she had met on her Valentine's night out in London the previous year. Trying not to act too much like a stalker, she found out where he lived and followed him to Tesco's one day, where she 'accidentally' bumped into him in the bakery section.

Striking up a conversation, they got on just as well as before. When he suggested going for a coffee, she eagerly accepted. That was in late January. By Valentine's Day they were dating, enjoying a lovely meal out at a country pub just outside Oxford.

During the meal, he asked her if she wanted to come to the Monaco Grand Prix with him in May. As part of his job, he got to attend three or four Formula One races a year, and for Kay, a lifelong fan, this was a dream come true. She had only been to a Grand Prix once before, at Silverstone as a kid, when her dad had taken her to see Nigel Mansell win.

Two days after Valentine's Day, she and Maddie had flown out to Tenerife, where they had spent a lazy week basking in the sun. It was the last day of the holiday now, and Kay felt relaxed, happy and ready to get on with her life.

She was unrecognisable from the person she had been less than two months ago. During the holiday, she had plenty of admiring glances from the men by the pool, and more than a few trying to chat her up in the evenings.

All of these offers she had rebuffed. She had high hopes for her future relationship prospects with Robert and certainly wasn't going to do anything to jeopardise them.

Things were looking up for Maddie, too. She had met a lovely young man from Newcastle while they were away, and they had arranged to meet up when she got back to Durham. Kay was pleased to discover that he seemed nothing like Glen or any of the other idiots she had endured. He reminded her more of the younger Kent.

It was fair to say that her experience with the angel had changed her life for the better. Kay felt proud of what she had achieved, even if it had been with the help of this mysterious divine intervention.

A little kick-start had been all she needed, just a helping hand to pick her up off the floor and give her the energy to dust herself down and start again. She knew she could easily have squandered the gift she had been given but she hadn't. She had used it wisely.

Now she felt like she could achieve anything. She may have been forty-three, but as far as she was concerned, she was as good as twenty-three again. There was still time to do everything she had wanted to do then. This time she would get it right.

Observing her from a sunbed on the other side of the pool, the angel smiled, pleased at another job well done. He was no longer projecting himself in her younger image but was now here in his true form and his real body, that of a man in late-middle age.

The angel never gave away anything about his true identity to the people he helped. It amused him to appear as an all-powerful being, appealing to his egotistical nature.

In truth, he was a mere mortal just like them, but coming from the future, with several decades of advanced

271

technology available to him, it wasn't difficult to make himself appear omnipotent.

He hadn't been entirely honest about the nature of the alternate universes Kay had visited. Long a believer in the multiverse theory, he had proven without doubt that alternate worlds could exist as a result of his earlier time travel experiments. He now knew how to create copies of the existing universe, but he certainly didn't have the power to delete them, nor would he want to.

After years of further experiments, he had now discovered how to travel not only between universes but to different points in time within them as well, hence his claim that he could be in any place at any time.

His work with Kay, Kent and the others was merely part of these experiments. His latest research was into the effects of transferring consciousness from an individual in one universe into another. Advanced developments in the field of measuring electrical activity in the brain also gave him a degree of insight into their thoughts.

By telling them the universe was merely a temporary copy, he intended to allow them to act freely, unconstrained by the usual rules that governed people's behaviour. He wanted to see what people would do, given free rein.

Then he could study the effects their trips back in time had, not only on their own lives but also on the world as a whole. How different might their lives be, and what ripples would flow out from the changes his subjects made?

Kay had been a fascinating subject. Unknown to her, all the different versions of herself she had created in the other universes were alive and well, except for the one that McVie had killed. If she had known this, perhaps it would have been some consolation to her to know that in that universe, Anna was alive and well.

Most of the other Kays were faring better. One effect of returning the original Kay's consciousness to the first universe meant that her copies had only vague memories of what they had done the previous day, and why. Even so, in most cases, they adapted to their altered circumstances well.

The first Kay, who had gone to Finland, continued her travels through Europe and never went back to Alan.

The version of Kay who had gone to the summer ball stayed with Kent, went to university and got her degree, carving out a successful presenting career with the BBC, just as she had hoped. She and Kent were married with three children.

The Kay who had stolen Alan's money on Valentine's Day had a life very similar to the original Kay. She had kept the house and divorced him several months earlier than before.

For the Kay who had travelled to Christmas Day as a child and had been to see Saint Etienne in 1993, there were no changes, either to her timeline or the world at large. She had more or less done on those days exactly what she had done the first time around.

None of this was known to this version of Kay, sunning herself by the pool, and nor did it matter. She was happy and her future was secure. She couldn't ask for any more than that.

The end…for now, but the series continues with My Tomorrow, Your Yesterday.

Reviews

Before you go, may I ask a small favour?

As an independent author, I don't have the strength of a big marketing budget behind me. I rely on word of mouth to spread the word about my books, plus genuine reviews from enthusiastic readers who have enjoyed the book. These help potential new readers decide whether or not to try a story from an author they haven't read before.

If you enjoyed the book, I would be hugely grateful if you would consider taking a few minutes to leave a short review on the Amazon website to let other readers know what you liked about the book. Every little helps, even if it is only a couple of short sentences.

Click here for the UK website:

https://www.amazon.co.uk/dp/B01N76YM5M/

Click here for the US website:

https://www.amazon.com/dp/B01N76YM5M/

The Time Bubble Collection

If you missed any of the earlier books in the series, please head over to my author page on Amazon where you can find them individually, or in box sets:

1) The Time Bubble
2) Global Cooling
3) Man Out of Time
4) Splinters in Time
5) Class of '92
6) Vanishing Point
7) Midlife Crisis
8) Rock Bottom
9) My Tomorrow, Your Yesterday
10) Happy New Year
11) Return to Tomorrow

UK Link:

https://www.amazon.co.uk/Jason-Ayres/e/B00CQO4XJC/

US Link:

https://www.amazon.com/Jason-Ayres/e/B00CQO4XJC/

My Tomorrow, Your Yesterday

Imagine living life backwards, one day at a time, from your deathbed to your birth.

When Thomas Scott wakes up in hospital on New Year's Day he has no memory of who he is or why he is there. Racked with pain from a terminal illness, death swiftly follows. As the days pass it becomes clear that the calendar is running in reverse.

Trying to find some purpose in life, he resolves to find out as much about his own personal history as he can. Learning of the death of his wife and an attack on his daughter, he prepares to make changes in the past to secure their future.

From middle-aged father all the way back to childhood, the passing years present all manner of different challenges as Thomas continues his journey backwards through the early 21st and the late 20th centuries.

This story is the ninth part of an epic series exploring the time travel genre in original and innovative ways. The novels follow the main characters from youth to middle age as they jump forwards, backwards, and sideways into alternate worlds.

UK: https://www.amazon.co.uk/gp/product/B00UDHAD0M/

US: https://www.amazon.com/gp/product/B00UDHAD0M/

Happy New Year

Amy's trapped in her own past - and it's always New Year's Eve.

Even before the time travel accident that sent her back in time, Amy hadn't enjoyed New Year. Now she's plummeting back through her life, living each one all over again. As she grows progressively younger, she is forced to confront some key moments from her life.

From dealing with an unfaithful boyfriend to trying to help her alcoholic mother, her attempts to make the most of her second chances meet with varying degrees of success.

As she grows ever more youthful, the reality of her impending mortality looms ever larger. Her only hope is to track down the mysterious stranger who sent her back through time, but he is nowhere to be found.

This story is the tenth part of an epic series exploring the time travel genre in original and innovative ways. The novels follow the main characters from youth to middle age as they jump forwards, backwards, and sideways into alternate worlds.

UK: https://www.amazon.co.uk/gp/product/B079H1RDMT/

US: https://www.amazon.com/gp/product/B079H1RDMT/

Return to Tomorrow

If you knew the future, would you change it?

In 1988, two young men know what life has in store for them.

Thomas Scott has lived his life twice before. At night he dreams about his wife-to-be and resolves to preserve the timeline so they can meet in the right place at the right time.

Ben Lewis was a middle-aged failure in 2020 before he was cast back into his eighteen-year-old body. Given a second chance, he intends to exploit it for his own selfish ends.

When the two meet in Oxford on a wintry January day, they soon clash. The more Thomas tries to prevent Ben from disrupting the timeline, the more he delights in doing the opposite.

A decade later, the scene is set for a final confrontation in the blazing heat of Ibiza at the height of the clubbing scene.

This story is the eleventh part of an epic series exploring the time travel genre in original and innovative ways. The novels follow the main characters from youth to middle age as they jump forwards, backwards, and sideways into alternate worlds.

About the author

Jason Ayres lives in the market town of Evesham with his wife and two sons.

Following a lengthy career in market research, he turned his hand to writing whilst bringing up his children. This included the popular *Stay at Home Dad* column in the *Oxford Mail*.

Encouraged by this success, he moved on to writing time travel novels, releasing *The Time Bubble* in the summer of 2014. This original and well-received story has since developed into an epic series which shows no signs of stopping.

Want to know more about Jason?

You can find his official website here:

https://www.jasonayres.co.uk/

Find him on Twitter:

https://twitter.com/TheTimeBubble/

Or check out his Facebook page for the latest news:

https://www.facebook.com/TheTimeBubble/

Printed in Great Britain
by Amazon

29455078R00164